A Candlelight Ecstasy Romance®

"PUT ME DOWN, GARAVELLI," SHE SAID THROUGH CLENCHED TEETH, "OR I'LL START SCREAMING."

"Go ahead," George dared, his face close to hers. "Dani, we can fight out here in the hallway, or we can discuss this civilly in your room."

"We have nothing civilized to discuss."

"Okay. If you insist, we'll be uncivilized," he countered. "I'll carry you inside, throw you on the bed and—"

"That's what you think!" Brave words, she thought, knowing he was prepared to kick the door down and carry out his threat.

"Lady, you've fought me since we were in first grade. It's time to settle our feud . . ."

CANDLELIGHT ECSTASY CLASSIC ROMANCES

CANDLELIGHT ECSTASY ROMANCES®

QUANTITY SALES

Most Dell Books are available at special quantity discounts when purchased in bulk by corporations, organizations, and special-interest groups. Custom imprinting or excerpting can also be done to fit special needs. For details write: Dell Publishing Co., Inc., 1 Dag Hammarskjold Plaza, New York, NY 10017, Attn.: Special Sales Dept., or phone: (212) 605-3319.

INDIVIDUAL SALES

Are there any Dell Books you want but cannot find in your local stores? If so, you can order them directly from us. You can get any Dell book in print. Simply include the book's title, author, and ISBN number, if you have it, along with a check or money order (no cash can be accepted) for the full retail price plus 75¢ per copy to cover shipping and handling. Mail to: Dell Readers Service, Dept. FM, 6 Regent Street, Livingston, N.J. 07039.

SWEET-TALKIN' LOVER

Anna Hudson

A CANDLELIGHT ECSTASY ROMANCE®

Published by
Dell Publishing Co., Inc.
1 Dag Hammarskjold Plaza
New York, New York 10017

Copyright © 1987 by Jo Ann Algermissen

All rights reserved. No part of this book may be reproduced or transmitted in any form or by any means, electronic or mechanical, including photocopying, recording or by any information storage and retrieval system, without the written permission of the Publisher, except where permitted by law.

Dell ® TM 681510, Dell Publishing Co., Inc.

Candlelight Ecstasy Romance®, 1,203,540, is a registered trademark of Dell Publishing Co., Inc., New York, New York.

ISBN: 0-440-18457-6

Printed in the United States of America

July 1987

10 9 8 7 6 5 4 3 2 1

WFH

Dedicated to Pappa Henry, Joanie, Harriett, Mary, the Prime Steer Restaurant employees, and, of course, to my husband, Henry, who let me order anything I wanted from the menu.

To Our Readers:

We have been delighted with your enthusiastic response to Candlelight Ecstasy Romances®, and we thank you for the interest you have shown in this exciting series.

In the upcoming months we will continue to present the distinctive sensuous love stories you have come to expect only from Ecstasy. We look forward to bringing you many more books from your favorite authors and also the very finest work from new authors of contemporary romantic fiction.

As always, we are striving to present the unique, absorbing love stories that you enjoy most—books that are more than ordinary romance. Your suggestions and comments are always welcome. Please write to us at the address below.

Sincerely,

The Editors
Candlelight Romances
1 Dag Hammarskjold Plaza
New York, New York 10017

SWEET-TALKIN' LOVER

CHAPTER ONE

"Bubble-butt? Is that you?" Danielle Brewster mimicked in a mock-surprise voice. "It can't be. You're a mere shadow of your former self! Where's the rest of you?"

Charles Du Bois chuckled at her wry imitation of how the folks in her hometown would greet her after she had been gone so long. During the past hour, Danielle had given a multitude of excuses for not leaving New York City to return to Williamsburg to help her parents close their home. Now, at last, she had given the real reason behind her reluctance to help her parents.

"Who cares how people you haven't seen for years remember you?" Charles reasoned. Time and distance separated Charles from his beginnings. At fifty-nine, he seriously doubted his high-school classmates would recognize him if he paraded naked down the French village where he'd been born.

"I shouldn't." But she did care, Danielle thought. Her hands automatically smoothed the nubby fabric of her suit skirt down her slender hips. "Mom said the farewell banquet to be given in their honor will have everything from imported baby lobster tails to zabaione." She groaned. "I gained ten pounds just listening to her talk about the banquet."

"You aren't going to double in size from one meal," Charles countered, watching her hands expand in girth. "Your mother sees food as a form of hugs and kisses, affection and love."

"Reward. Got a good report card? Here, have a box of Twinkies to celebrate." Danielle gracefully sank to her knees beside Charles, who was seated on a chair in her living room. Modestly she tugged her skirt to the calves of her slender legs. Despite her present predicament, her dark eyes brimmed with humor. "And punishment, too. When I was a roly-poly toddler I used to sneak into the bathroom when Mom was taking a bath. I remember being fascinated by the toilet's swirling water. I'd drop my mother's lacy underthings into the toilet and squeal with laughter as I watched them disappear. You know, I can almost hear my dad saying, 'You were a naughty, naughty girl. Go straight to your room without dinner.' Food was withheld if I was in disfavor."

Laugh wrinkles creased the corners of Charles's eyes. Danielle must have been a handful as a child, he thought. Her spunky, uninhibited behavior had singled her out from his other students the moment she had walked into his gourmet cooking class. He'd been preparing to demonstrate the intricacies of making cassata alla siciliana. After class, she'd patted her hips and requested a recipe for low-calorie chocolate and whipping cream.

Danielle snapped him back from his reverie by saying, "Good grief, Charles, do you realize what my reward for sharing the honor of graduating at the top of the senior class with George Garavelli was? Dad paid my tuition to chef's school. How's that for the ultimate food reward?"

Charles stroked her silky dark hair as she wrapped one arm across his knees and buried her cheek against his lap. He'd heard her mention George Garavelli on other occasions. Danielle and George had shared more than scholastic awards. Evidently, from the time George hit her with the ball while they were playing dodge ball in first grade and loosened Danielle's front teeth, they'd been not too friendly competitors. Raised as an only child of indulgent parents, Danielle saw few reasons to share glory with anyone, much less George.

"Aren't you lucky that your parents didn't raise George?"

She lifted her face, her dark eyebrows arching in puzzlement.

"They'd have sent George to chef's school as well," he teased, tweaking the tip of her nose with his thumb and forefinger.

13

"You aren't taking this seriously," Danielle complained lightheartedly. Charles invariably could make mincemeat of major problems. "My mother made plane and hotel reservations. How am I going to graciously refuse her invitation?"

"You aren't. Think of it this way," he suggested tongue in cheek, "you can provide those colonials with more excitement than they've seen since the American Revolution."

"Meaning?"

"You've been to London to see the Queen, haven't you?"

"The Queen's chef," Danielle corrected. Following his line of thought, she tried to imagine herself attending a formal ball at Windsor Castle. Her half-formed mental picture fizzled. Glitz and glitter had little personal appeal, but she knew the snapshots of the castle that she had sent her parents were impressive.

"And what about Kuwait?" Charles prodded her memory. "How many residents of Williamsburg have dreamed of being captured and thrown into the harem slave quarters of an Arabian sheikh?"

"Quarters that have been transformed into a nursery with separate kitchen facilities for the sheikh's children. And I was invited, not kidnapped."

Charles gave a typical Gallic shrug. "Who's to know?"

"I'd know. On the surface, our world trav-

14

els sound exciting, but you and I know how seldom we get beyond the kitchens. Hired help and royalty seldom mingle socially."

"Bah! You *practical* Americans," Charles complained with an affectionate tug to a strand of her hair. "Sour cream made from cottage cheese. High-fiber bread made mostly with sawdust. Soybeans for protein instead of prime beef."

"Don't get me started on nutrition," she warned. After mastering the art of gourmet cooking, she had devised tasty substitutes that eliminated salt, cholesterol, and sugar without destroying the aesthetic appeal or changing the flavor. "What does my specialization have to do with visiting my parents?"

"Simple, my thorny little American rose: exaggerate."

"Lie?"

"Never lie," he protested, making a tsking noise. "Be mysterious. Toss out a few red herrings to tempt their palates."

Danielle shook her head, but felt an odd sense of exhilaration. "Fish stories eventually stink."

"Only if improperly prepared." Charles lifted the gold-handled cane from beside his chair. "Take this, for instance. We both know why I use a cane."

"Arthritis." She watched as he appeared to lithely rise from the chair. Only a momentary wrinkling of his brow disclosed the cost of his quick movement. Short, slight, and bearded,

15

Charles exemplified continental charm. He stopped in front of the fake fireplace and swung his cane in a wide arc.

"Do I look like an elderly man with health problems?"

"Of course not." She gave him an impish grin. "You're as dapper as Maurice Chevalier."

Feet spread, he leaned heavily on his gold-tipped cane, nodding as though he'd proven the point he was making. "An illusion. On the inside, I creak and groan with age, but I don't let everyone see that. Carrying a cane enhances the illusion that I'm a debonair Frenchman, while serving a practical purpose. Is the cane a lie?"

"No, it's a necessity," she agreed, feeling as though she were back in his classroom listening to a lecture.

"So? When you return to your provincial little hometown, on the inside you can feel vulnerable, but," he extended his cane, jauntily flipping the golden tip toward her, "on the outside you'll be an intriguing, sophisticated woman of the world."

Danielle grasped the cane's handle. Slowly Charles brought her to her feet, drawing her closer. His hand reached to her and cradled her heart-shaped face. She was such a charming bundle of contradictions. Slender on the outside, fat on the inside. Insecure and confident. Demure and impudent. Tenderhearted and assertive. Like a fabulous gem, she had many facets.

"You create magnificent illusions daily with your nonfattening creations, *ma chérie.* Your patrons expect their palates to be tantalized with your epicurean delights. Would you disappoint them?"

"No."

"Do you beat them over the head with your practical nature by listing the amount of calories in each serving?"

"No. The customers get what they expect. Food beautifully prepared but low in calories." She could see admiration and pride glinting in his pale blue eyes.

"Give your parents and your old friends what they expect," he concluded.

Danielle turned her lips to the dry palm of Charles's hand and placed an affectionate kiss there. "It isn't that simple."

"Make it simple."

"But Charles, most of the women my age are married with two point five children." She heard his low chuckle and smiled. Marriage wasn't an unfamiliar topic. She had tactfully broached the subject during the past six months while they had tested the recipes for a low-calorie cookbook she had written. He'd graciously avoided a direct reply, but she had heard him humming strains from a May–December song. "I'm twenty-eight."

"Ancient. You'll be shopping for a golden cane any day," Charles concurred in jest, then added seriously, "I've offered you a business partnership. Anything more would destroy a wonderful friendship."

Charles had difficulty denying Danielle's smallest request. He loved her. Not in the frantic passionate manner that marked his youth, but calmly, quietly, as befitted his maturity. They were friends, good friends, the best of friends. But in moments of weakness such as now when her self-confidence was fragile, he was tempted to take her beyond the boundaries of friendship. What man his age wouldn't be flattered to have such a lovely, youthful woman as his wife?

Selfishly, he had flirted with the idea of dropping on bended knee and proposing. Yet the knowledge that Danielle would have to help him back to his feet dispelled any illusions he had of being husband material to a woman thirty years his junior. He couldn't stop the hands of time for himself by robbing Danielle of her youth.

He was content with their arrangement.

Discontent, Danielle sighed as he affectionately kissed her head in a fatherly manner. "You could solve this problem for me, then we'll discuss a business arrangement."

"Father two children before this weekend?" He ran his finger from the bridge of her nose to the tip. "There are some problems a play-tonic relationship can't cure."

Danielle groaned comically at his glib de-

18

scription. "Play for me? Tonic for you? Sometimes I think it's the other way around."

"Exactly the reason for keeping everything status quo. Why spoil a wonderful friendship with marriage?" Eyes gleaming with mischief, he added before she could answer, "You could tell everyone we're living together."

"That isn't exactly true." They'd been continuously in and out of each other's pockets while he had edited her cookbook, but living together sounded . . . mentally she searched for an accurate word. Wicked? Sophisticated? Cosmopolitan? Mysterious? She pondered Charles's suggestion, beginning to like the idea.

She couldn't produce a husband and two children on such short notice, but she could create a dish suitable for the Williamsburg palate. At twenty-eight, many of her parents' cronies considered her a spinster. "Spinster" brought to mind shriveled prunes—plums dried by the sun. Could she concoct a dish from prunes? Something sweet and tart and rich, she mused, her mouth involuntarily watering.

Her imagination soared with the idea. Washed, pared down and pitted, the prune was a nutritious fruit. A pinch of cinnamon, a packet of sweetener, a dollop of luscious fat-free whipping cream, and . . . *voilà!* A dessert the citizens of Williamsburg would adore.

From the golden flecks in her eyes, Charles could tell he'd piqued her interest. "A sprin-

19

kling of paprika can make a world of difference to the taste of baked chicken."

"Or prunes," she mumbled, caught up with her idea.

"Non, ma petite. You're more like a spring chicken than a prune." He chuckled as he tilted her head from one side to the other as though carefully inspecting a piece of poultry. "True, you've lost weight, but your skin is flawless." His critical eyes gave her a comprehensive sweep as he stepped back, holding her ar arm's length. "New feathers, perhaps? That would bolster your self-confidence?"

"Clothes?" Her weakness for fattening foods had changed over the years to a love of fashion. A shopping spree was a nonfattening reward system.

"October in Virginia is warmer than autumn in New York."

She spun from the light hold he had on her and charged toward her bedroom. Charles smirked. With his guidance she had made her decision. His lips sagged a little when he realized how much he would miss her when she left.

"Charles"—she poked her head around the doorway—"while I'm away you will take your vitamins, won't you?"

"Oui, chérie, by the handful."

"And you'll—"

"Brush my teeth and comb my hair—what's left of them," he quipped good-naturedly. "It will be difficult, but I can survive without your fussing."

"I don't fuss!" Danielle shouted, returning to her walk-in closet. "I care. There's a difference."

Unable to resist teasing her, he crossed the living room to her doorway and said, "Make certain you remember everything I've taught you."

"I won't be preparing food. Mom said the furniture is on its way to Florida. No cooking utensils at her house. She made reservations for me at the MacGruder Inn."

"I wasn't referring to your culinary expertise."

Danielle tossed several transitional outfits on the bed and glanced at Charles, smiling. He taught her everything from playing bridge to art appreciation to philosophy. "If Dad finds a fourth for bridge I promise not to overbid my hand."

"No grand slam bidding with ten high card points? Impossible!"

"You rigged the deck, giving me twelve spades and a low diamond," she recalled. "You're the last person I'd have suspected of cheating." Her accusation was accompanied with a low chuckle.

"You're a most stubborn woman. You were supposed to drop out of the bidding when I reached seven hearts. Who'd have thought you'd bid seven spades? You knew you had one loser." He shrugged in typical French fashion. "Only an American would have such nerve."

Without remorse she countered, "A great defense strategy. I lost the hand, but I won the rubber. I hope this half-baked plan of ours works as well." She pointed to the pile of clothing. "Not one *femme fatale* outfit in my wardrobe."

"Perfect excuse to go shopping, isn't it?"

"Perfect," Danielle responded. "Want to come along?"

Certain his friend would spend hours satisfying her appetite for fashion, Charles shook his head and leaned heavily on his cane. "Age does impose limitations."

"Mother booked an early-afternoon flight on Friday. Will I see you before I leave?"

"But of course. I'll ride with you to the airport." A wink as broad as his grin accompanied his eloquent, Shakespearean farewell, " 'Parting is such sweet sorrow.' "

"See you later." Danielle blew him a saucy kiss.

With a three-hundred-and-sixty-degree twirl of his cane, Charles departed, making certain her door was locked.

Danielle bundled the assortment of dresses and rehung them in the closet. Her stomach knotted, then growled hungrily. Certain a few suitable dresses would pacify her psychological need for food, she picked up her purse and strode briskly to the door.

A short while later Danielle was at her favorite store browsing through a myriad of clothes racks and her hunger pangs diminished. She needed exactly the right cocktail dress for her parents' farewell banquet. Automatically, she reached for the darker-toned dresses—she'd worn black, brown, and navy throughout her teenage years. Now she could openly admit to a secret longing to wear vibrant colors.

Danielle couldn't remember who had first told her black made her look thin, but she'd believed the myth. Ridiculous, she mouthed, limiting her choice to brighter hues. A limousine looked the same size regardless of whether it was black or white.

Her best friend, Buffy Sinclair, had encouraged Danielle to wear red to accentuate the positive and eliminate the negative aspects of her figure flaws. Buffy, being tall, thin and flat-chested, had diametrically opposite figure problems. She would drink milkshakes and lose weight.

Making a mental note to call her lifelong friend the moment she arrived in Williamsburg, Danielle selected a white cashmere sweater dress. A discriminating shopper, she realized the bateau neck, graceful roll-up sleeves, and waltz-length, drop-waisted skirt would enhance her feminine curves. She fingered the soft, fluffy natural fibers. It was luxurious, not too dressy, but not informal. Simple, but sensuous. Perfect for the occasion, she decided. Buffy would heartily approve of her choice.

She had started toward the cashier when a striking silver-starred and black-feathered cocktail dress caught her eye. Outrageous high fashion, she mused, her steps slowing to a stop. She clutched the sweater dress closer to her chest, knowing it was the suitable choice. Although she'd disliked Charles referring to Williamsburg as provincial, it was a long way from this type of flamboyant attire. Her eyes were as bright as the glittering dress as she folded the sweater dress over her arm and plucked the feathered creation from the rack. If one dress could curb her appetite, two could destroy it.

Danielle could taste sweet, sweet triumph a few minutes later as she slipped on the spangled garment. Arms raised, fingers securing her stylishly cut, shoulder-length hair atop her head, she critically inspected her image in the three-way mirror.

The dress, she thought, was a statement of how she had changed, what she was and who she had become. At least on the outside, she silently tacked on with perverse honesty. But, as Charles had reminded her, how would anyone know differently? Without climbing inside her skin, no one would realize she hadn't changed.

Disrobing, she glanced at the price tag dangling from the long sleeve and swallowed in shock.

"Illusions are expensive as hell. I could buy a month's groceries for that amount." Her shoulders dismissively lifted a fraction of an inch. "It will be worth every penny spent, every calorie unconsumed."

Late the same evening, after telephoning her parents, informing Charles of her purchases in glowing description, and packing, Danielle was surprised to find she was definitely looking forward to the trip. As she slid between satin sheets, a low moan of satisfaction passed through her lips.

A short respite from New York City's hustle and bustle would give her the breathing space she needed to make a decision regarding Charles's latest career proposition.

He absolutely refused to accompany her on another trip to the home of the diet-conscious wealthy and famous. Planning, construction, and testing her cookbook was satisfying, but often tedious work. Charles dreamed of opening a restaurant. Something swanky and secluded, yet extravagant and unique.

His proposal piqued her interest, but she wasn't certain blasé New Yorkers would patronize a gourmet low-calorie establishment. After all, a New York strip steak was king and rich sauces were the queen of the Big Apple, she had argued.

Find another location, Charles had countered, undaunted by any stumbling block she placed in his path. Earlier, on the phone, he had told her to check out her hometown as a possible location. She'd laughed. Belgian waffles and restaurants specializing in colonial cuisine were typical there. Yes, there were a few exceptions . . .

An unwelcome image of George Garavelli swam behind her closed eyelids. His family owned and operated Garavelli's Italian Restaurant. Growing up, George had worked there part-time, when he wasn't devoting his energies to outshining her. While other teenagers rushed from school-sponsored activities so they wouldn't have to stand in line for Garavelli's pizza, she scrupulously avoided the place as though it were the birthplace of ptomaine poisoning.

The worst quarrels she'd had with Buffy revolved around George. Buffy, like the rest of the female population, had had a king-sized crush on him. The girls had nicknamed George the Italian Stallion; Danielle privately called him a horse's ass. Buffy oohed and aahed; Danielle gagged.

And George? He blithely ignored both of them socially. He dated what Buffy disparagingly called "cutesy butts."

However, that didn't stop Buffy from voting for George in the class presidency election. Danielle had fervently campaigned against him, wishing she could be unscrupulous enough to stuff the ballot box. Instead, she had stuffed her stomach. She'd almost overdosed on burger doodles because of George Garavelli.

As graduation had loomed ominously on the horizon, she confided to Buffy her secret fantasy: she wanted to become a health inspector so she could slap a giant-sized B sticker on Garavelli's front window.

Tucking the sheet under her chin, Danielle chuckled over those long-forgotten memories. George Garavelli was probably married and had started his own student council by now. Too much pasta had probably changed his athletic build. He was fat and balding; she was chic and sophisticated. Poetic justice was sweeter than a double-dip of spumoni ice cream.

CHAPTER TWO

"Mom! Dad!" Danielle enthusiastically greeted her parents, giving her father a special hug and her mother a kiss. The prospects of taking early retirement and settling in Florida must be giving both of them a new lease on life, she thought as her eyes swept over them. Thanks to jogging five miles a day and a metabolism that could burn the calories of a German chocolate cake in two hours, her father appeared in his prime. His near-white hair and receding hairline were the only clues to his age. Unfortunately, her mother had fought the Battle of the Bulge and lost. But, nevertheless, the care she'd taken with her skin and her good taste in clothes made her an attractive matron. "You both look great!"

Dan and Ellie Brewster glowed with pride. Public displays of affection slightly embarrassed them, but their one and only child could do little wrong.

"Let me look at you," her mother said, scanning Danielle from her shiny hair to the tips of her equally shiny black patent-leather shoes. "You look good enough to eat. Speaking of eating, have you been starving yourself?"

"Shame on you, Mom," Danielle replied, uninjured by her mother's candidness. From her mother's viewpoint, anyone under a size sixteen was leaning toward anorexia. "Nutrition experts don't starve."

Laughing, Dan took his two favorite women by the arms and directed them toward the luggage carousel. "Your mother worried all night about not being able to cook for you. I swear, she'd have unpacked kitchen utensils from the moving van if the movers weren't halfway to Florida."

"The phones at the house are disconnected, too, or I'd have made other arrangements," Ellie added. "Did you eat on the plane?"

"No, the flight was too short."

"Are you hungry?" both parents chimed in unison.

Danielle laughed and shook her head. Some things in life remained constant. She'd been a good girl to come home on short notice, therefore her parents felt obligated to show their appreciation by feeding her. "I can wait until dinner."

"Uh, yes, about dinner," her mother stammered. Her eyebrows knitted in consternation. "Dan, you tell her."

"Me!" Dan protested. "You're the one who accepted the invitation. Do your own dirty work."

"But he was your boss. I couldn't refuse his

invitation." Ellie gave her daughter an apologetic look.

Her father consoled his wife with an affectionate pat on the hand. "Your mother keeps forgetting I'm retired. No more command performances to please the boss."

"Mom, don't worry about dinner. I can call room service at the hotel."

Her hand clamped between her dad's arm and his ribs as Dan flinched. Her mother's eyes changed from apologetic blue to icy blue. "It's his fault you can't stay at the house. He didn't rent a trailer big enough for two sets of bedroom furniture."

"The car can't pull a load that heavy."

"Hey!" Her parents jaw-boning back and forth hadn't changed, either. They loved each other, but both of them were too stubborn and proud to admit they'd made a mistake. Danielle knew that flaw in her character had to be genetic. "I'm not complaining. Don't worry."

"Well dear, I didn't want you to sit at the hotel or go to a near-empty house, so I called Buffy."

"Great! Thanks, Mom. Buffy and I can—"

"Buffy has a date she couldn't break," Dan interjected, "but she invited you to join them."

"Insisted," her mother said when Danielle began shaking her head.

"That's sweet of her, but—"

"Buffy said she'd never forgive you if you

didn't at least join them for a drink at the Trellis Restaurant. Personally, I think she wants to show off her new boyfriend." Ellie sniffed with mild indignation. "She's one step up on you, daughter. She caught herself a man who's been in Atlanta the past few years. When are you going to introduce us to some lucky young man?"

Avoiding a direct response, Danielle pointed to the luggage coming through the chute. The farewell gag-gift Charles had placed on her fourth finger caught light and sparkled brilliantly. "There are my bags."

Danielle silently groaned when she saw her parents' eyes locked on her finger.

At the airport in New York, Charles, in his usual grandiose manner, had presented her with a two and a half carat cubic zirconia ring. He told her with mock gravity that he couldn't provide her with two point five children, but he insisted she wear the ring as a talisman. It would ward off evil spirits and provide her with magical powers. Any time she felt her confidence shaking she was supposed to kiss the stone for good luck, make a wish, and think of him. She had laughed at his whimsical superstitious nonsense, then solemnly vowed to wear it as a token of their friendship.

At the moment, observing both of her parents' jaws drop to their respective chests, she wished she could swallow it.

31

"You're engaged and you didn't tell us?" Ellie asked in a hurt voice.

"Who's the lucky man?" her father boomed, obviously delighted.

She couldn't lie to her parents. "Charles gave it to me," she answered truthfully.

Before Danielle could explain, her mother wailed, "Charles? You mean Mr. Du Bois? My God, child, he's older than your father. You can't marry *him.*"

Loyal to the bone marrow, Danielle huffed, "I'm over twenty-one, mother. As a matter of fact, I'm twenty-eight."

"But, he's *my* age!"

Dan stepped between the two women. "Now Ellie, you're overreacting. I seem to recall you gushing over Charles last Christmas when we were in New York."

"I don't gush!"

"The hell you don't. I was green with jealousy and you loved it. Ask Dani. She'll confirm it."

Danielle grabbed her luggage from the conveyor belt, hating being a pawn in their bickering matches. Bickering made her nervous; it always had and they were well aware of how it affected her. She fervently wished they'd call a halt to their verbal warfare during her visit. "Stop it, you two. People are beginning to watch us. One more disparaging word about Charles and I'll go to the reservation desk and book a return flight."

"See what you've done, Dan?"

"Me?"

Dropping her luggage with a loud thud, Danielle hugged both of them, whispering, "It's a friendship ring, not an engagement ring. Please don't fight."

"We weren't fighting," Dan said, squeezing his wife's shoulders to end the turmoil. "We think it's wonderful that you're . . . going steady."

Danielle chuckled as she brushed a grateful kiss on her father's cheek. Her talisman must be working, she thought, because suddenly all three of them were giggling like schoolchildren.

During the drive to the MacGruder Inn, Danielle told her parents the circumstances surrounding the ring. Although they tried to hide their relief, she could tell Charles wasn't the man either of them would pick for her.

After checking into the luxury hotel and making certain Danielle's rental car was on the parking lot, Ellie pressed a bag of chocolate candies into her daughter's hand. "You never know about room-service food. I just hate the thought of you sitting here in your room, all alone on your first night home."

"If I promise to eat elsewhere will you quit worrying and enjoy yourself tonight?" Danielle asked.

Ellie nodded; Dan reached into his pocket. Danielle shook her head sharply. Shrugging toward his wife, he dropped a kiss on his daughter's head. "New York makes women too damned independent," he griped.

His eyes belied his gruffness. He was proud of his Dani.

"I'll see you tomorrow at home," she promised, adding, "not too early."

"I'll have doughnuts and coffee waiting for you." Reluctant to go, Ellie gave her daughter another hug. "Don't forget Buffy. I gave her your room number. If you don't show up she'll probably come and get you."

Buffy would, too, Danielle thought as she closed the door behind her parents. The rest of the world viewed her friend as a timid mouse. But she knew how ferociously adamant Buffy could be.

Slowly, without realizing what she was doing, Danielle ripped the corner off the package of candy as she contemplated the idea of Buffy having a man in her life. *Envious?* She popped two morsels of chocolate in her mouth. She wasn't jumping up and down with joy—especially when she considered her parents' reaction to the prospect of having Charles as a son-in-law.

The chocolate started melting.

Deciding she wouldn't know whether or not she was happy for Buffy until she'd met her boyfriend, Danielle centered her thoughts on how defensive she'd been with her parents. She thought she had outgrown the desire to please them. Knowing her mother was extremely protective, she doubted that any man would be good enough. Last Christmas Danielle had interpreted her mother's gushing as approval. Come to think of it, that's when she had first mentioned the possibility of marriage to Charles.

She swallowed, smiled, and tossed four more candies into her mouth. Danielle wasn't going to allow her mother to use her hard-won independence as a rug to wipe her feet. If her parents had their way they'd probably choose someone like George Garavelli for her to marry.

Groaning, she ground her teeth together and chocolate coated her taste buds. Lord have mercy, she'd slipped into another old habit. She tossed the package on the night-stand. She was beyond the need to appease her frustrations with sweets.

"Eat to live, not live to eat," she muttered, disgusted with the idea of losing sight of the first rule of dieting.

A quiet knock at the door drew her attention. Certain Ellie must have ordered a basket of cheese and wine delivered to her room, she groaned aloud as she crossed to open it. Back in control of her appetite and her destiny, she decided to send the food back to the kitchen. At least in Williamsburg she didn't have to worry about opening the door without knowing who was in the hall.

She flung the door open wide. "No, th-th-anks," she stammered, unable to stop her mouth soon enough. She blinked twice, positive her subconscious was playing tricks on her.

George Garavelli stood within touching distance. Stunned, she barely noticed the shaggy, colorful spider mums in his hands. A lock of his dark wavy hair had fallen over his brow as though he had nervously raked his hand through it shortly before he'd knocked. His black eyes danced with mischief and his lips parted. Danielle heard the low, husky chuckle that curled the toes of Williamsburg's female population directed exclusively toward her.

George hated blind dates. If Mario hadn't dangled the possibility of combining business with pleasure he would have flatly refused. But, knowing how temperamental a chef could be when provoked, he had agreed to picking up an out-of-towner and meeting Mario and his new girlfriend at the Trellis Restaurant. Undoubtedly, Mario's new love had to be Buffy Sinclair.

Only by strangling the stems of the flowers in his hands had he managed to keep from laughing with glee when Danielle opened the door. Her untimely refusal gave him an opportunity to pay her back for being stuck-up throughout their competitive years in school.

"Don't New York women wait to be propositioned before saying no?" he asked, his voice laced with amusement. Certain she'd slam the door in his face, he assumed a nonchalant pose by leaning against the door frame while sticking his foot inside the room.

His preposterous question completely shredded the glossy shell of sophistication she had acquired in New York. Her heart hammered against her ribs, her stomach twisted into a knot, and her mouth watered as though she'd eaten the entire package of candy. But her agile mind kicked into high gear.

"In New York we don't open our doors to strange men."

George had been around clever women enough to know she'd baited him. He was too elusive to fall into her verbal trap by responding, I'm no stranger. Uh-uh. He wasn't going to let her whittle him down to size by retorting, No, but you're definitely strange.

"By midnight we'll be intimately reacquainted," he quipped with a self-confidence he definitely lacked when he was around Miss High and Mighty Brewster. Her chin tilted upward, putting her perk nose in a position he well remembered. Determined to lower it, he let the petals of the bouquet brush against her breasts.

Her dark eyes dropped to the flowers, partly to hide her reaction to his seductive promise, and partly because of her physical response to his audacious gesture. Her nipples grew taut inside her lacy bra. Certain George would see the effect through her silk dress if he withdrew the flowers, she accepted them, clutching the blooms to her chest.

"You have the wrong room, but thanks for the flowers," she said, recovering her wit. The thought of him having to go emptyhanded to pick up his real date tickled her. Her dark eyes gleamed with smug satisfaction as she silently chortled. "Now, if you'll excuse me, I have a dinner engagement."

"No mistake," George countered, inching inside the threshold. Her spicy fragrance tantalized his nose. "Buffy's friend, Mario, asked me to be your escort."

Automatically, Danielle stepped backward to avoid having the flowers crushed between her chest and his. Buffy wouldn't fix her up with George Garavelli. Of all people, her best friend knew Danielle hated him with a passion.

Inside the room, George closed the door behind himself.

Silence sizzled between them.

A billion packages of candy inhaled in a steady stream couldn't calm Danielle's nervous stomach. Eat, eat, eat, her subconscious pounded, matching the accelerated beat of her heart. His black bedroom eyes oozed sex appeal. She wanted to erase his cocky smile with kisses. George Garavelli was the last man on earth who should have had this effect on her. Damn it, he was the boy who had nicknamed her Bubble-butt! Why wasn't George fat and bald as he was supposed to be?

Unaware she'd been steadily moving backward, she was appalled when she felt the bed touch the back of her knees. An egotist right down to his highly polished loafers, he would probably think she'd accepted his proposition. With a sharp gesture she motioned toward the chair near the window.

"I'm not ready for a dinner date," she said much too breathlessly.

"You look fine," he said as he sat in the chair.

Admit it, George, he thought, she looked better than fine. A few more pounds arranged in the right places like they used to be and she'd be perfect. Her backward retreat had whetted his instinct to give chase. Chasing after Danielle Brewster must be a difficult habit to break. Lord knew he'd pursued her since first grade, to no avail. With a saucy flip of her silky hair and an upward tilt of her nose, she had left him standing there every time.

She was too prissy for an Italian kid from the wrong side of town. As a teenager, he had tried everything in his meager repertoire to impress her. Miss Better Than Thou was too elegant to step foot in his parents' unfashionable restaurant. At school, she had steadfastly ignored him, or worse, vehemently opposed him.

She'd eventually become his obsession. He'd done everything within his power to prove to her that he was her equal. By the time they had graduated, sharing academic honors, he'd been ready to throttle her.

When she graduated and left Williamsburg it had been a blessing in disguise. With her nowhere in the vicinity he could concentrate on building a career. How ironic that they'd both chosen different areas of the same business, he mused. While she'd gone to her fancy chef's school, he'd attended a state university, majoring in food services. And, according to the pictures her mother had shown around town, Danielle had flitted around the world while he'd served his apprenticeship in New Orleans.

Different paths to the same goal: recognition in the food industry as being the best in the gourmet food industry.

An unwelcome shiver of delight ran up Danielle's spine as she watched his eyes linger on her figure. Oh how she would love to fling his hateful nickname in his face. Little did he know she'd survive on air to keep him from being able to make disparaging remarks about her size.

She wouldn't give him the satisfaction of refusing to be seen with him. Nor would she fall all over him like other women. George Garavelli had always aroused strong emotions in her. His masculine appeal had intensified over the years. Her defenses were pathetically weak. In the fold of her skirt she rubbed the stone of her talisman against her thigh.

I wish he'd fall for me.

I wish she'd fall for me, George mused, wishing for the impossible. Settling for being in her exalted presence for longer than it took for her to spit in his eye—not that she'd lower herself to such a common level—he said, "Mario booked reservations for seven o'clock. Unless you want to change clothes, we'd better leave." The thought of Danielle changing clothes in front of him brought a rakish grin and a devilish twinkle to his eyes. "We could be a bit late if you'd rather I called room service for a bottle of champagne to celebrate our getting back together."

"Back together?" Danielle hiccuped, instantly regretting sounding like a hollow echo. She was tempted to decorate him with flowers when she heard him chuckle. He'd baited her and she'd responded in a puerile manner. Adopting a haughty, sophisticated air to cover her momentary relapse, she stated, "We've never been together. Sorry."

"Me, too." He rose from the chair, chilled by her icy glare. Unable to bend his pride enough to grovel for a mere dinner date, he said, "I'm ready when you are."

Ready? For what? Dinner? Celebrating? Her face flamed at other intimate options her wild imagination provided. She refused to ask, too afraid she'd be willing to follow his lead wherever it took them. Flustered beyond measure, she glanced down at the flowers. The stems and leaves had suffered, but they gave her an immediate excuse to go in the bathroom and splash cold water on her face.

"Let me take care of these," she murmured, fleeing into the bathroom.

Damn her persnickety hide! Even the welcome-home flowers from Buffy that he delivered weren't good enough for Danielle Brewster. Princess Dani must be accustomed to orchids, he silently sneered. Wondering why he was setting himself up for an evening of verbal slaps, he plunged his hands into his pockets. Her attitude hadn't changed. She'd always thought she was too good to associate with him.

After rinsing her face, Danielle looked in the cabinet for a vase. The sink was too small and shallow to hold the large bouquet. The wastecan was made of some sort of metal but it wouldn't hold water. The flowers would drown in the tub. Stubbornly refusing to admit defeat on such a small matter, she carefully arranged them in the only place left that perpetually held water. Before the evening ended, she'd ask Buffy for a vase.

One glance in the mirror assured her applying makeup wasn't necessary. Her dark eyes shone brightly; her cheeks were pink. Her hair swung neatly around her shoulders. Taking a deep breath, she opened the door.

Directly outside the bathroom, George waited patiently at the door that led into the hallway.

"Let me get my purse."

George inhaled a whiff of her perfume as she walked past him. Curious as to what fragrance she wore, he stepped into the bathroom to see if the perfume bottle was on the counter. His lips compressed into a thin line.

She'd dumped the flowers into the toilet! The wastecan wasn't adequate?

His fingers balled into a fist. She'd gone too far. He had put her up on a pedestal since she'd worn her hair in banana curls, but she needed to be taken down a peg or two. Once and for all he was going to teach Danielle Brewster a lesson—and it wasn't going to be one she'd file in a recipe box!

Pasting a smile on his face, he stepped to the door and held it open for her, bowing at the waist like a good little lackey. His hot Italian temper got the best of him. He asked in a pseudo-sweet voice, "What fragrance of *toilette* water are you wearing?"

Danielle smiled at George's attempt at a French accent. It had taken her a while to get used to hearing Charles call cologne by its original name. She stepped in the hall, replying over her shoulder, "Obsession."

"I should have known," George muttered, shutting the door harder than necessary. His lousy French accent had taken the sharp edge off his pointed remark. Sarcasm ill suited him. Out of habit, he cupped her elbow in his hand, matching his steps to hers.

His touch had the same effect on Danielle's nerves as lifting electric beaters out of gooseberries. Splatters of goose bumps sprayed over her from her neck downward.

43

He had never touched her, she realized. Her eyes widened in amazement and were drawn to his face.

George dropped her elbow as though it were a hot utensil. His palm burned with an intensely pleasurable sensation. He'd been extremely cautious until now to keep his hands to himself. As an adolescent, the mere thought of holding her hand had driven him crazy. Had? What he felt at the moment defied rational thought. He couldn't attribute the tremor in his hands to anger. Regardless of where she'd thrown the flowers, she still had an invisible hold on his heart.

To cover her reaction, Danielle gaily said, "I'm surprised we aren't dining at Garavelli's. Your family is still in business, isn't it?"

"Yeah, but Mario interviewed for the position as head chef at the Trellis. I'm trying to convince him to rejoin Garavelli's."

"Rejoin?"

She passed through the lobby unaware of anything other than being the direct object of George Garavelli's attention. He held the door for her, but made certain there was plenty of room to avoid having her brush against him.

"Mario is a distant cousin who worked for us part-time a while back." He inhaled the crisp autumn air deeply into his lungs. It didn't help clear his memory of her perfume. But he did feel on safer ground discussing

44

Mario. "I understand you've made a name for yourself in the food industry."

Flattered, she smiled warmly. Had Princess Fergie personally thanked her for a scrumptious lo-cal meal, she couldn't have been more pleased. She wanted to tell George about the cookbook that would be getting national publicity within the next few months, but was hesitant to toot her own horn.

"Thanks. I manage to keep the creditors off my doorstep."

"Bat those big brown eyes of yours in their direction and they'd forget why they were there."

Danielle felt light-headed. Two compliments in less than a minute. One more and she'd swoon like a seventeenth-century miss and thoroughly disgrace herself. Charles was charming; George was devastating.

"New York bill collectors have a reputation of being merciless," she demurred, hoping he'd continue.

"Fishing for compliments, Ms. Brewster?" he asked, gesturing toward his car.

She chuckled, then took them back on safe ground by shortening his word. "Fish. That's what's at the heart of my business."

"Brain food. Now if you want heart, try a thick, creamy clam sauce poured over linguine or a wedge of cheesy pizza. Mmm. That's Italiano!"

That's heart trouble, she mused, her eyes mesmerized by the tip of his tongue as it circled his lips. She wondered if his kisses would electrify her. Considering her heated response to having him merely touch her, she felt certain she could fry eggs in the palm of her hand.

"I don't recall ever seeing you at Garavel-li's."

"That's because I've never been there," she admitted, unable to explain further. She didn't want to spoil their amiable truce. His frown alarmed her. Impulsively she added, "But I used to snitch bites of Buffy's takeouts."

George laughed as he unlocked and opened the passenger door. "Refusal to enter your arch-rival's encampment?"

"Something like that," she hedged.

Tucking her full skirt beside the velour seat, he whispered, "And here I thought you had a reason for calling me Garlic Mouth."

"Who told you that? Why, I—" Danielle clamped her lips shut. She had, in a moment of justifiable outrage, used that exact name. He'd branded her with a name that had never been forgotten. "Care to trade Garlic Mouth for Bubble-butt?" she offered sweetly.

CHAPTER THREE

"Reservation for Garavelli, please," George said to the hostess.

Danielle focused her attention on the autumn flower arrangement on a mahogany drop-leaf table in the foyer to keep from staring at George. He hadn't apologized for nicknaming her, neither had she. Surprisingly, when he'd smiled and repeated it, Bubble-butt sounded closer to being an endearment than a hateful nickname.

The hostess checked the reservation list and the seating chart, then handed George a white slip of paper. "Follow me, please."

Danielle kept a sharp eye out for Buffy as they wound through the tables. She didn't want to miss seeing the expression on her friend's face. Buffy would die from shock. When they arrived at a cozy table for four, where all of the seats were empty, she gave George a puzzled glance.

"Thank you." Holding the chair for Danielle, he explained, "Mario left a message saying they'll join us later."

47

They were seated in the front dining room which overlooked the cluster of colonial shops across the street. Gaslights lit the entrances. Danielle smiled, recognizing her favorite candy store. She'd spent a fortune in there salving each puncture to her wounded pride that George had administered. Smiling, she realized the hunger she felt had little to do with eating.

To divert her thoughts from the wayward path they persisted in following, she spread her napkin in her lap. "I wonder why they're going to be late," she said with a note of concern.

"The message didn't say." George seated himself across the table from her. His dark complexion deepened several shades in color when his knee bumped hers beneath the linen tablecloth. "Sorry."

She wasn't sorry. Each time he casually touched her it was heavenly.

To her amazement, he ordered an exceptionally fine champagne. With his Italian palate, she expected him to request a full-bodied, robust burgundy. He'd mispronounced *toilette* earlier, but even Charles couldn't have said the lengthy French name of the champagne better. After he'd tasted his selection, nodded acceptance, and watched as Danielle's glass was poured, he settled comfortably in his chair.

"Wipe the startled look off your face, would you? I may not have trained in New York or traveled abroad, but the university did insist on properly training future chefs." He grinned and raised his wineglass. "Shall I propose a toast?"

Danielle nodded.

"To bittersweet memories. May the future hold only sweet dreams."

"To sweet dreams," she replied as the rim of her glass touched his. Tiny bubbles tickled her nose. Thanks to Charles's persistent chiding, she'd learned to swallow her giggles. "Excellent choice."

"You'd have turned your nose up if I'd ordered Chianti. Champagne is a seductive wine, don't you agree?"

Irked by his second reference to her being snobbish, she replied, "I'll bow to your expertise on seduction. Mine is limited."

She had mentally added a couple of tablespoons of vinegar to her response, but her voice lacked the biting edge she'd intended. The wistful quality her ears detected disgusted her. While he'd been gaining his expertise in seduction, did he think she'd been sipping expensive wine from a sterling silver goblet, thumbing her nose at a long line of suitors? Stuffing herself with homemade pastries was closer to the truth. She'd collected recipes while he'd collected volumes of little black books that contained women's names and phone numbers. Silently she scoffed at the image.

George watched her wrinkle her nose. He

49

considered her seductive powers limitless. Sitting this close to Danielle made him feel like a starving man in front of a banquet table with his hands tied behind his back. He wanted to snap the civilized bonds of restraint shackling his hands and reach across the table.

Oh Lord, what he could do to the provocative pout of her lips. Their natural color reminded him of ripe cherries. Tart and sweet. He wanted to taste her sweetness, gorge his appetite until he no longer craved her.

He licked the residue of champagne from his lips to dispel the image. The dry flavor brought him back to reality.

"You're far more seductive than wine, twice as addictive," he flattered sincerely.

His black eyes slowly caressed her face and throat, the silky fabric covering her breasts. Danielle was powerless to stop the pleasurable sensations coursing through her. He'd earned his reputation. She felt like a recalcitrant mare being gently prodded toward an inevitable destiny.

She pinched her thigh—hard. She had to break the spell of his devilish black eyes or she'd be another mare in his overstocked herd.

"Flowers, champagne, and compliments. Does that work on all your women?" she asked caustically.

George watched her fingers clamp around the long stem of her wineglass.

"Don't," he warned, knowing she was perfectly capable of tossing the contents in his face, then breezing through the door. She had smashed a double-dip ice cream up his nose when they'd been pre-schoolers without a moment's remorse. She hadn't changed. "Buffy expects you to be here when she arrives."

Aware of his eyes shifting to her right hand, she raised the glass in mock salute and sipped her wine. She had outgrown spiteful behavior. She would cool off her growing desire by pouring the contents of her glass in her own lap before giving him the satisfaction of knowing he was getting to her.

"In answer to your question, I'm not interested in what appeals to all women. I am interested in discovering what appeals to you."

She swirled the wine on her tongue; its effervescence exploded her taste buds. Him, she could have answered candidly. But no, she wasn't going to let him in on that little secret.

"Why? Because we grew up in the same town? Face it, George, we've been natural enemies from day one—like red squirrels and gray squirrels, hawks and chickens."

George thoughtfully rotated the stem of his glass between his thumb and forefinger. He wasn't the Don Juan she'd given him credit for, but he wasn't a callow youth, either. On a subliminal level, she had responded to him. Each time they made eye contact it had the

51

same effect as lighting a match to brandy fumes. Flames leaped between them. She wasn't impervious to his touch, either.

"Do natural enemies congenially share a glass of champagne?" he bantered.

"No. They must be smarter than we are. They avoid fighting by keeping in their own territories."

Shifting the subject to safer ground, he asked, "Did your parents tell you that they've become Saturday night regulars at Garavelli's?"

"No, they didn't mention it." They had listened to her gripe about "that Garavelli kid" often enough to know what her reaction would have been. The Brewsters eating at Garavelli's would have been the equivalent of the McCoys dining with the Hatfields. "I'll have to admit, I'm astounded. Neither of them mastered the art of twirling spaghetti on a fork."

"They solved the problem by ordering tortellini. Dan prefers red sauce, Ellie white sauce." His lips twitched as he remembered how they argued back and forth, unable to convince each other as to which was best. "Ellie enjoys showing the photographs you send her."

Knowing how her parents habitually disagreed with each other accounted for his stifled grin, Danielle deduced. Her discomfort vanished when he revealed his curiosity regarding her whereabouts. Pleased, she fished, "Been keeping tabs on me?"

"A good chef knows the ingredients of any dish he prepares," George teased.

"Hmm." She sipped her champagne, puzzled by his response. Her voice matched his in teasing quality as she quipped, "I didn't know goose was an Italian dish."

His husky chuckle sent shivers of awareness through her. He leaned forward; his dark eyes smoldered, clearly indicating his intentions. A pinch of sensual undertone spiced his reply. "We're no longer arch-rivals. I have no intention of cooking your goose. I want us to be . . . colleagues."

Danielle could have sworn she heard the pawing of horses' hooves. On her lap, her fingers lightly gauged her pulse. What she'd heard was heated blood percolating through her veins. Lacing her fingers together, her good-luck ring grazed against her middle knuckle. She wondered if she was doomed to a life of men offering friendship when she wanted more, much more. Tempted to make the same wish twice, she polished the fake stone against her silk skirt. Why waste wishes? She'd be leaving in four days.

"Why the grim look?" He held his hand toward her, palm upward. "See, no buzzer."

She placed her right hand on top of his and offered, "Four days of friendship to erase the bitter memories."

"Rome wasn't built in four days," he purposely misquoted. She had changed his choice of words from colleague to friend. What he had in mind wasn't friendship. "Any chance of you returning to Williamsburg on a permanent basis?"

Danielle trailed her fingers across the crease lines in his hand until only their fingertips touched. "Charles Du Bois suggested I consider Williamsburg's potential for another restaurant."

"Charles Du Bois?" He'd recently read a newspaper article about the retired chef *extraordinaire*. He recalled the basic facts aloud, combining what he'd read with what Ellie had told him. "Third son of some French royal family? He couldn't inherit so he left France to make his own fortune. His reputation is worldwide. Was he the man with the fancy cane in the pictures you sent home?"

"Yes," she beamed, delighted that he knew about Charles's background and reputation. "He was teaching a class I enrolled in my first year in New York. After I graduated, I became his," she paused, searching for the right title. She was more than an assistant, but less than a partner. "Protégée."

George would have considered Charles as heavy competition if he hadn't seen a picture of the old geezer. Charles was twice Danielle's age. Having been a mentor for several of his younger cousins, he understood Danielle's relationship with Charles.

"French royalty in the heart of Colonial America?" he quipped.

"No problem. Charles could charm an American eagle from his lofty nest." She chuckled, remembering her father admitting to being jealous of Charles. "Mother is an active member in the Daughters of the American Revolution. Charles broke through her New England reserve in nothing flat."

The timely arrival of Mario and Buffy kept the niggling doubts George was beginning to feel from being expressed. He hated to openly admit it, but a descendant of the aristocratic Du Bois family outclassed a Garavelli son. Some women did prefer older, experienced men. Charles's continental charm had worked on Danielle's mother. What about the daughter? Was there more to this mentor/protégée relationship than friendship? He'd have to find out, but not in front of another couple.

George stood. While the two men clapped each other on the back as though they hadn't seen each other in years, Danielle watched Buffy nervously glance from George to herself.

"I didn't know!" Buffy mouthed, crossing her heart.

Danielle winked and smiled.

"Danielle Brewster, meet the originator of the finest pizza crust on the East Coast. Chewy . . ."

"But not too chewy," Mario augmented.

55

"Crusty . . ."

"But not too crusty."

"Light . . ."

"Never, never too light. I'm not in the waffle business," Mario protested, his dark eyes bright. "Poor Giorgio. He makes great sauce, but lousy crust."

"All the more reason for you to decide in favor of Garavelli's," George coaxed. He kissed the tips of his fingers in a typically Italian gesture. His eyes turned toward Buffy. "Good to see you again, Buffy. We've missed you at Garavelli's."

"Perhaps no longer," Mario said as he raised Buffy's left hand. A small, lovely diamond in a Tiffany setting twinkled as merrily as Mario's eyes. "She's graciously agreed to become my bride."

"It's beautiful, Buffy." Danielle took Buffy's hand between both of hers. Her dearest friend's face radiated joy. Mario had to be the right man for Buffy. That was good enough for Danielle. "I'm happy for you."

"We're late because Mario wanted to ask my father's permission before he made an offer I couldn't refuse," Buffy explained with pride, without apology.

Mario's Old World courtesy further endeared him to Danielle. In the days of quick marriages and quick divorces, she felt it boded well for Buffy's future happiness.

"Good thing you didn't have to ask Dan and Ellie, Danielle's parents. You'd have been three days late while they debated the pros and cons of their darling daughter marrying a cook," George teased as the other couple seated themselves.

"Chef," Mario corrected indignantly.

George countered, "That depends upon which offer you accept."

"Humph! I worry more about telling the Garavellis my decision than which job to take. Should I decide to take a position outside of the family business, World War Three will commence." Mario cast his cousin a smile, then said to Danielle, "Your parents' disputes are civilized compared to our family. On my first date with Buffy I made the mistake of taking her for dinner at Garavelli's. Isobella, Giorgio's mamma, asked Buffy how she felt about babies." He gave his cousin a sly smile and added, "It seems her sons are sadly lacking in carrying on the family name."

Buffy blushed; George's eyes snapped, demanding silence from his cousin.

Dismissing his cousin's reaction with a casual wave of his hand, Mario continued his game of oneupmanship by teasing, "Perhaps Isobella fears her Garavelli stallions are geldings?"

"We haven't been put to pasture yet, cousin." George gestured for the waiter, knowing Mario would razz him until his ears turned beet red. He felt certain Mario was getting even for the earthy comments Mario had been subjected to during the past month.

After introducing Buffy, Mario had refused to bring her back to the family's restaurant. "Let's order."

Buffy picked up her menu and leaned to the side. Whispering, she said to Danielle, "I couldn't wait until tomorrow for you to meet Mario. He was supposed to ask George's older brother, Tony, to escort you. What gives with you and George? When we came in, you two looked like salt and pepper shakers."

"Long-overdue friendship."

"Friendship?" Buffy hissed in disbelief. Her blue eyes rolled from her menu toward the ceiling. "The Garavellis have strictly Old World views. Men and women are *never* friends. Isobella wants babies; Giorgio probably wants revenge. Believe me, he hasn't forgotten how you campaigned against him every time his name was on the ballot. Friendship? Not where you're concerned. Try pillow friend, the Italian version of mistress."

Mario brought his fiancée's hand to his lips. "Nice ladies don't whisper."

"I was just telling Danielle how much I was looking forward to being your missus," Buffy agilely transposed.

While the waiter took their orders, Danielle stared at George over the top of her menu. Tempted to solve her problem by requesting soup, salad, two entrées, and the biggest dessert on the menu, she quelled her hunger pangs by trying to solve her dilemma.

Was revenge the reason George had been

such a sweetheart all evening? Had he tricked her with his glib compliments? Those soulful black eyes of his had been sending steamy messages in a universal language that made a mockery of the word "friend." Yeah, and she took the bait, hook, line, and sinker, she silently grumbled. Eat worms and die full!

"I'll have baked flounder," she said when the waiter moved beside her. She needed all the brain food she could eat. She must have been addled to believe George had honorable intentions.

"I hope the flowers we had delivered make up for being late," Mario said apologetically to Danielle.

"Actually, I intercepted the delivery man and hand delivered them myself," George said, his eyes narrowing as he remembered what Danielle had done with the flowers she thought he'd given her.

"Aha, so you took credit. Careful, Danielle," Mario warned, "beware of Italian stallions bearing gifts."

Danielle strangled a laugh through stiff lips and returned the dirty look George was giving her. This was more like old times, she thought. Thrust and parry. Gouge or be gouged. "Thanks for the flowers. I did think George bought them. Buffy, would you remind me to stop and get a vase?"

"Oh, dear, I should have thought of that when we placed the order. I hope they don't wilt."

"They won't," George replied, intensely disliking the thought of where she'd put them when she believed they were from him. Now, since the bouquet hadn't come from him, she planned on retrieving them. "She thought they were from me and disposed of them accordingly."

Buffy giggled. "The eternal spring?"

Danielle nodded, shrugging her shoulders helplessly. George must have seen where she'd put the flowers and assumed she purposely tossed them in there as some sort of petty revenge.

Let him assume the worst, she decided. He always had.

Her earliest memory of him was at the ice cream parlor. Her mother had taken her and Buffy there for a treat after a dance recital. Like other little kids, they were roughhousing when they weren't supposed to be. Accidentally, Buffy had pushed her against George. It wasn't her fault he'd rammed his nose into his lime sherbet. Yes, she and Buffy had broken into gales of girlish giggles, but he would have laughed, too, if he hadn't been on the wrong end of the ice cream cone. Instead, he'd assumed the worst and screamed and yelled, demanding Ellie spank her prissy little daughter.

Well, eating worms at twenty-eight wasn't funny, either. But she would order worms for breakfast, lunch, and dinner before she explained to George that she and Buffy had had a similar flower problem as kids and come up with the same solution. "It worked for you."

Patting Mario's hand, Buffy whispered, "I'll tell you later. Inside joke."

Which left him out in the cold, George thought, reminded of the jealousy he'd felt as a youngster over Danielle's close friendship with Buffy. He curbed an impulse to shake his fist in the air and demand an explanation. He should have controlled his hot temper and not let on that he knew what she'd done with the flowers, he silently lamented. To make up for his lapse in manners, he asked, "Danielle, what's this Ellie told me about you being the author of a fabulous cookbook?"

More worms? She wasn't going to open her mouth and swallow the hook this time. She was going to be on the other end of the fishing pole for a change. Unaware of doing it, her nose tilted upward. "You wouldn't be interested."

"Fishing again?" he teased in an effort to establish the rapport they'd shared before Buffy and Mario arrived.

"You can't catch a stallion with a worm," Mario razzed. "Try using a rope—as in around his neck."

"Her arms around my neck would be more effective," George suggested, giving Mario a butt-out glare. He felt perfectly capable of botching the evening without help from his cousin.

"A ring through the nose, perhaps?" Buffy

said, joining the verbal play. "Or maybe one through his ear would suffice? Dani, don't you think a gold earring would improve his rakish good looks?"

Seeing how Mario and Buffy had both pounced on him, she replied soft-heartedly, "Nothing could improve his looks."

Mario groaned dramatically while Buffy sighed and shook her head.

George could have jumped for joy. Danielle didn't mind dishing it out herself, but she wasn't going to let the others dig in. His admiration of her grew. He hadn't thought that possible.

Throughout dinner, both George and Danielle centered the conversation around who had been doing what since they'd graduated from high school. Mario had met most of them at one time or another at Garavelli's.

Danielle knew Charles would have chided her for giving an unglamorous summation of what she'd been doing. Funny, she mused as she declined ordering dessert and opted for black coffee, she'd had the perfect opportunity to really impress George and hadn't felt inclined to take it. Her former arch-rival had touted her success as though he had invented the artificial sweetener she used in her recipes.

By the time the two men had haggled over who was going to pay the bill, with George winning by handing the waiter a charge card,

Danielle was wondering if Bubble-butt had been a product of her imagination.

"Mind if I drop by your parents' house to-morrow?" Buffy asked. "We need to have a long talk before you leave."

Danielle grinned. Buffy's blue eyes bouncing between the two men left little doubt as to what they'd be discussing. "I'd love it. Bring a box because there will probably be photographs you'd like to have."

"Sure you don't want us to take you back to the hotel?" Buffy whispered. Seeing her friend shake her head, she reminded, "Don't forget to stop and get a vase."

"No point in her buying one," George said, overhearing Buffy's reminder. "I can't take credit for the flowers, but I can provide her with a vase."

After they were under the green canopy leading into the Trellis, Mario pounded George on the back and said to Buffy in a loud stage whisper, "See why he owns the restaurant and he wants me to run the kitchen? It took me weeks to get you to my apartment and it's only taken my cousin hours to finagle Danielle into going to his place."

George could have cheerfully put his knuckles against his cousin's front teeth. His hope of Danielle understanding how the Garavelli men tormented each other with rib-ald comments dimmed as he watched her shoulder blades stiffen. Buffy was shooting pointed daggers at him, too.

"The shop across the street is open," Danielle gritted between tight lips. A mental picture of being alone with George in his apartment, with him focusing his sexual charisma on her, left her without doubt as to how she'd respond. Unless she changed her destination immediately, she'd be yet another notch on his bedpost. Giving Buffy a quick hug, she said for George's benefit, "I'll get one there."

"I owe you one, cuz," George said, giving Mario's hand a knuckle-busting handshake. When Danielle darted across the street without him, Mario tightened his grip.

"Oh, I'd say you and your brothers are still ahead on the scoreboard," Mario replied, totally unrepentant. George tried to shake his hand loose, but Mario clung tenaciously to his fingers. "Bring Danielle to Garavelli's before she leaves town."

Letting his hot temper get ahead of his common sense, George replied, "Her parents' farewell party is booked for Sunday. Danielle won't have the problems you let Buffy encounter."

Mario roared with laughter. "You're underestimating your brothers. By the time the party rolls around they'll have your mother oiling up the white shotgun. It will be a formal occasion, won't it?"

"If you don't let go of my hand, you won't have a trigger finger." Danielle had disappeared into the shop. He hated the idea of chasing after her, but Mario had given him no alternative. "Now."

Danielle moved in a direct course from the front door of the curio shop through the back exit. The alley behind the store provided her with a way to make her way to the rear entrance of the candy shop. Should George decide to follow her, he'd be inside the first shop while she exited from the front of the candy shop and caught a cab.

Tempted by the aroma of fresh chocolate to stop long enough to stock up on calories for the evening, she mouthed, "I don't need candy. And I sure as hell don't need George Garavelli!"

In less than five minutes she was in a cab headed away from the historical area and toward her hotel. Angry with herself for letting George get through her defenses, she muttered self-recriminations until she noticed the cabbie watching her in the rearview mirror. Undoubtedly he thought he had an escapee from the loony bin in the backseat.

Danielle wholeheartedly agreed.

She should have listened to Buffy. George wasn't interested in friendship. He wanted revenge. Revenge was a powerful motivator. She'd made him miserable, not that he hadn't deserved it. Now it was his turn.

Danielle paid the cab driver and stomped through the lobby and up to her room. She inserted the key, still muttering to herself when the earth tilted, spinning dizzily as she was lifted from her feet.

"Put me down, Garavelli!" she gasped defiantly, clutching his lapels to regain her equilibrium. "I'm going to count to five, then I'm going to scream bloody murder."

"Go ahead," he dared, clamping one of her arms against his chest and the other in his hand. She'd slap him for his audacity. There was no mistaking the fire in her eyes. "We can duke it out here or pretend to be civilized and continue this discussion in your room."

"Pretend?" she sputtered. "You're the barbarian. Put me down!" She paused between each word for emphasis. "We have nothing *civilized* to discuss."

"Okay. If you insist, we'll be uncivilized. I'll carry you inside, throw you on the bed, strip off—"

"You'll go to hell first." Danielle seldom lost her temper, but when she did it was enough to make most men run for the hills. From the tight grip on her arm she realized he was prepared to kick the door down and carry through with his threat.

"Lady, I've lived there since I first set eyes on you. It's time to settle our feud."

CHAPTER FOUR

George unlocked the door, opened it, then kicked it shut after carrying Danielle across the threshold. Flailing her arms, she felt as light as a feather and equally ineffectual.

She bounced twice when he dropped her on the bed. Her romantic nature battled with reality. An awareness of feeling deliciously feminine internally fought with her indignation.

As a child she'd dreamed of a strong, courageous knight in shining armor swooping her into his arms and carrying her away to his castle. Strength, back then, was imperative. Most underdeveloped teenage boys would have staggered under her weight. And yet, as an adult she resented having brute strength be the determining factor in an argument.

Her head ruled her heart as she gasped, "If I were a man you wouldn't toss me around."

"Right on! If you were a man I would have punched your lights out for the potshots you've taken at me."

George stormed to the far side of the room,

getting as far away from Danielle as possible. Rumpled and mussed, she was tempting as hell. He'd wanted her shell of cool disdain cracked, but he hadn't planned on discovering a hot molten inner core.

For some unexplainable reason, his obsession to make her undeniably his increased tenfold. He wanted to stake his claim in primitive fashion—by physically dominating her. His fingers clenched into fists and he shoved his hands in his pockets. Physical domination would be an ignoble victory that would enable her to climb back on her pedestal and look down at him.

"Don't bite off more than you can chew," she blasted, swinging her legs over the side of the bed. Shoulders braced, chin raised defiantly, she glared at him.

"Dammit, Danielle, we've verbally sparred for years. Would you feel better if you slapped my face? Come on," he goaded. "Take a swing. Get it out of your system."

"Brawling is beneath my dignity. Physical violence doesn't solve anything," she said coldly, letting the chill in her voice cool the miniature explosions occurring where he'd touched her.

His dark eyebrows rose. Her haughty iciness made him livid. He wheeled around and faced the window to keep from closing the gap between them. The urge to kiss that delectable mouth of hers until she was capable of only sweet murmurs made him say derisively, "Beneath your dignity? Figures."

Thrice he'd implied she was a snob. Once she could pass off as a casual remark. The second reference had irked her. But a third comment had her bounding from the bed, grabbing him by the arm and spinning him around.

"That's three. Out! Get out of my room. I'm no snob and I never have been."

Catching him unaware, he momentarily lost his sense of balance. Before he could stop the propelling force, he collided against her. The tight rein he held on his desire to kiss her senseless frayed to a single slender thread.

"I should leave," he agreed. His fingers shimmied down her arms. Loosely he circled her wrist, drawing her hands behind his back. "Touching you is like dropping icicles into a deep fat fryer."

"I'm the ice?" Ten years ago she'd have automatically assumed she was the fat. She could have broken the light manacle hold he had on her. Should, she told herself, feeling her anger dwindle toward nothingness. His crooked smile and the coloring high on his cheeks obliterated rationality.

"Ice and fire," he replied ruefully. "Cold water I understand. God knows I took enough cold showers after watching you strut down the school corridor."

"You shouldn't say—"

"I know. I'm offending your sensibilities.

But I think our vinegar-and-oil relationship needs a good shaking up."

"Shake me and I can guarantee a swift kick to your shins." Her threat held no rancor. Her anger had calmed. Which wasn't surprising, she thought, knowing her own temperament. George Garavelli was the only person in the world she'd carried a grudge against.

She wondered if Buffy had confused who was the person hellbent on revenge. Danielle silently admitted to having human flaws. Seeing the man she'd declared open warfare on being humbled held a certain amount of appeal.

"I'm more inclined to keep an eye on your knee than your toes," he countered, amusement sneaking into his dark eyes. "One swift blow and I'd be incapacitated."

"I'm incapable of landing a low blow. We've had our disagreements, but I've always fought fair."

"Fair?" he chided. Was it fair that she'd changed from a precocious, bratty girl into such a lovely woman? Was it fair that she'd tormented him, snubbed him, when all he'd wanted was to impress her? Was it fair that she'd been a major stumbling block in any relationship he'd had with other women? She didn't know how to fight fair.

"You've had unfair advantage from the time you were in banana curls," he replied, his voice husky.

"Is that so?" Disbelief laced her words.

"You'd have knocked my front teeth out during the dodge ball game in first grade if I'd had any teeth there to begin with. I'd be wearing dentures if we'd been in third grade."

"That was an accident. Frankly, it scared the hell out of me."

"Why? Scared Dan and Ellie would become the owners of Garavelli's after they sued the pants off your family?" Her taunt lost its effectiveness when her voice grew breathy as his fingers twined in the hair at her nape.

Reflexively, her neck bent to one side, capturing the underside of his wrist against her pulse point. Her dark hair fell to one side, exposing the graceful curve of her neck and shoulder. She felt his heart skip a beat and saw the black centers of his dark eyes expand. Knowing he wasn't immune to her brought her heart slamming against her chest.

His thumb sensuously flicked the lobe of her ear back and forth. "No. I thought I'd hurt more than your . . . dignity when you landed on the seat of your pants."

"You're impossible." Danielle laughed softly.

"Not for you," he returned, watching her reaction. "We're alike in many ways. Anything is possible between us."

"You just told me how different we are, remember?"

"Granted, sparks fly between us." He released the hold he had on both her hands, crooked his forefinger and placed it beneath her chin, raising her lips to his. "But they make a lovely, lovely glow."

Unable to resist his vital magnetism, she raised on tiptoe. The fleshy pad of his thumb skimmed across her mouth, momentarily settling on the thin crease, then gently nudged her lower lip until it parted voluntarily. *Could long-standing enemies become lovers?* she wondered. His lips hovered over hers, tempting her to discover the answer.

"No woman has ever inflamed my senses the way you do," he whispered.

"Giorgio . . ." Why she'd used the Italian version of his name, she didn't know. Without her lips touching his, she knew he'd taste of coffee and Grand Marnier. A rich, intoxicating combination blended with his secret flavor she longed to taste.

He was irresistible; she was past resisting. He knew it; she knew it.

Each prolonged second heightened his anticipation. She would be amazed to know how much he relished prolonging the inevitable, he thought. Hearing her speak the name only family members used added to the moment.

Danielle's body quivered against his. An inch closer and she'd be touching him from head to toe. She wished . . . oh how she wished. A curious sense of heavenly bliss seemed to surround them. Her hands languidly lifted to his shoulders. His arm circled her and granted her unspoken wish.

"You want me to kiss you, don't you? Tell me, Dani."

He could have spoken the question, or she could have read his lips. She didn't know. Her sole attention was on his mouth.

It took less than a second for her to silently answer. What shocked her was knowing she'd wanted his kiss for more years than she cared to remember. She gave a tiny protest of denial.

"Yes. Give me that much, sweetheart. I've stormed the Bastille and slayed the dragon, so reward me. Tell me you want my kiss."

From the deep recesses of her mind, Danielle pulled a long-hidden fantasy to the present. Her hands climbed across his muscular shoulders, up the back of his neck, into the slight waves at the crown of his head. Her first kiss. She'd dreamed of it—with him co-starring in the fantasy. She'd mentally blocked recognizing his dark features, but now she knew.

"Um-hmm."

Her lips hummed with the tiniest vibration against his. Shafts of pleasure swept through him, binding her closely as his forearm tightened in response. His hand held her head in place. He sealed her lips to his by parting them with the tip of his tongue. Slowly he entered. Nothing in his past experience prepared him for being inside of her.

Sweet. She tasted incredibly sweet.

Danielle tasted coffee, liqueur, and his

73

laughter, his witty charm, his intelligence, his desire—a heady combination that was all Giorgio Garavelli.

George swirled his tongue deep inside of her, unable to control his pent-up desire. He'd imagined kissing her. Once in kindergarten when he'd wrestled her to the ground to keep her from biting him. Again in junior high when he'd sprouted his first manly hair. Later, in high school, when he'd lost his virginity. His imagination was black and white and muted grays compared to the vibrant colors exploding in his mind.

Her lips gently sipping his tongue, the small kittenish sounds he heard, the feel of her hands pressing against his back brought to mind another bolder image of being deep inside of her. His fingers wadded the silky fabric below the back of her waist to keep from ripping the fragile cloth to shreds. He wanted her naked against him. He strained against her to relieve the building ache that circled his heart and shot downward.

He was the one whose nickname, Italian Stallion, held a certain aura of sexual expertise, but one touch, one kiss threatened to destroy his image. He couldn't think of a single technique he'd used previously to excite a woman into uncontrollable passion. Dani reduced him to the adolescent kid who didn't know what to do next.

Realizing he was rotating her hips against his arousal, he reacted like an inexperienced teenager and shifted her into a less-revealing embrace. In ten seconds or less he knew he'd be throwing her on the bed, hiking her skirt and thrusting inside of her unless he stopped immediately.

"Holy Mother of God," he groaned, pulling his mouth from hers. His mind seemed instantly paralyzed by an acute sense of loss. He couldn't think; couldn't speak. He further disgraced himself by panting like a kid.

When his brain began to function, he mumbled, "I should have known. I kiss you and look what happens to me. Now I know what the hell I've been afraid of all these years."

Stunned by the recrimination she heard in his voice, Danielle stumbled back until she collapsed against the bed, sinking to a sitting position. She appealed to the same higher being that George had spoken to when he'd pushed her away. He was afraid of her. He had good reason to be, she agreed. Had she actually been clawing at his jacket as though she wanted to tear his clothes from his body? Had her hips pressed against him, unwillingly causing a natural response from him? For heaven's sake, one of his kisses had changed her from a circumspect woman into a . . . a nympho!

Mortified by her behavior and his calling a halt to their first kiss, she grabbed a pillow and buried her burning face into its softness. "Get out. Please, just leave."

George stood rooted to the carpet in her

room. He couldn't leave and he couldn't stay. If he left, she'd refuse to see him again. If he stayed, maybe, just maybe he had a chance to get control of his emotions.

He glanced down at his trembling hand. Shaking like a kid. She'd gotten to him. His whole body felt as though it had gone up in smoke, leaving a charred emptiness.

"You won," Danielle conceded, her words muffled. "Please, take your victory and . . ."

Realizing how ridiculous her begrudging concession was, George laughed. In a crisis situation he'd always responded in that manner. The pillow Danielle had been holding collided into his midsection. Doubling over, he laughed harder.

He'd won? Hell, she'd hoisted him up by his own sword!

"Stop! Don't you dare laugh at me!"

She grabbed for the other pillow, wanting to pound the stuffing out of him. He had poked fun at her forever. She wanted to stuff the entire pillow right down his throat to muffle the spiteful sound. Before she could raise it to throw it with force, she found herself sprawled beneath him.

Danielle fought. Arms swinging, legs kicking, head twisting, she tried to get away from his hateful grasp.

"You're going to hurt yourself. Stop," he ordered to no avail. "I'll leave, but dammit, you're going to listen to me first."

Danielle wanted to cover her ears and sing

76

la-la-la at the top of her lungs the way she had as a six-year-old when someone was going to say something she didn't want to hear. Physically fighting George was only leading to further humiliation.

Aware he'd straddled her to protect himself, she went limp. Eyes squeezed shut, she waited for him to get off her. He didn't.

"Open your eyes, Danielle Brewster," he commanded in a curious tone that piqued her interest. She obeyed. "What do you see?"

"You. Get off of me. You weigh a ton."

Automatically she tugged at the arm he held stretched over her head. George didn't budge an inch.

"I'd make you promise to lay there peacefully, but I know the minute I let go, you'll disappear. Like it or not, I'm going to say my piece."

Danielle shut her eyes as though it would affect her hearing. His throaty chuckle made her squirm, but she kept her lids closed. Teeth clamped, her lips thinned into a flat, straight line.

"You have a nasty habit of selective listening and overreacting," he commented.

She couldn't let that remark pass. "Thanks. I'll give you a character reading by mail, otherwise we'd be stuck here for years. I do want you out of here."

George grinned at a particularly pleasant thought. Who'd have believed that under her prissy, ruffled exterior a real hellcat lurked?

Beneath the *dignity* she'd referred to earlier was an extremely passionate woman. He'd kissed her, but she'd kissed him back with ardor unmatched by any woman he'd known.

Danielle took a deep breath in preparation for a scathing list of her shortcomings. He probably had them emblazoned in his memory. What was taking him so long to get started on his tirade? She peeked through her sooty lashes.

"Stop smirking and start talking," she said, expelling the air trapped in her lungs.

"Did you hear me say that I knew what I'd been *afraid* of all these years?"

"Yes. So what? You want to—"

"Afraid of what you do to me, sweetheart," he continued as though he hadn't heard her. "Do you know I've avoided touching you for years because I was scared of what it would do to me?"

"Scared?" she repeated, confused.

"Petrified. Terrified. You scared the hell out of me."

"Why?"

"Because of how I knew I'd react. All you did was kiss me and you brought me to my knees." He grinned ruefully. "That's a hell of a horse trick."

Opening both eyes wide, Danielle stared at him as though he'd lost his mind and was babbling like a lunatic. She'd thought he'd been repulsed by her responding as though she were starved for sex. Now she realized his recriminations were aimed at himself, not her.

George snorted, releasing one hand long enough to make a sweeping gesture in the air. "Flowers, champagne, gourmet dinner to show you I could match your worldliness, and I wind up making a horse's ass out of myself with one kiss. You're disgusted. That's why you're kicking me out of the barn."

Tempted to remind him of who sent the flowers, she watched his tongue roll around in his cheek and burst into laughter. Only George, impossible scoundrel that he was, could make light of a painful situation by poking fun at himself. He hadn't wasted words by making a vow of undying, unrequited love that she wouldn't have believed. He'd made her laugh when she'd wanted to die.

"Gelding would be too good for me," he added, rolling to the side of her when he heard her gasping for air. "I shouldn't expect a woman with discriminating taste to even consider looking at me."

Turning on her side, Danielle took a long, hard look. She started at his polished loafers and followed the sharp crease of his trousers up his long, muscular legs. She heard his breath stop as her eyes lingered on the thin leather belt at his waist. An inch at a time, button by button, she lazily studied him as though he were a stallion she might be interested in purchasing.

She perused his mouth. "Open up."

"You'll have to take my word. I'm not too old for you and my hard mouth will soften with the right woman holding the reins."

"Hard mouth?" No, his was seductive, soft, persuasive, she mused, uncertain of what he meant.

"A hard-mouthed beast refuses to be led around."

Her dark eyebrow raised. "Yep. You're a hard-mouthed beast," she agreed emphatically. "But a magnificent beast. I rather enjoy looking at you, although admittedly I'm not much of an equestrian."

Steam would have been coming from his ears if they'd been a pressure valve on a pressure cooker. She was one hell of a woman, he thought, appreciating her compliment and her sense of humor.

"Does that mean you might consider kissing me—knowing I'm head-shy?"

Imitating the haughty accent of the snob he'd accused her of being, she replied airily, "A woman of taste knows a thoroughbred when she sees one. She's willing to overlook minor temperamental flaws knowing that with time and proper training she'd be booking a winner. Until that time, she's willing to endure a certain amount of—"

"Pawing?"

"Hmm. If you must."

He tentatively placed his hand on the feminine curve of her waist. His thumb skittered across her lowest rib. He pulled her close to him. "I must."

Heart racing, she shuddered when his hand cupped her breast. His eyes never left hers. His exquisite caress was far from anything she'd classify as pawing.

"That feels good," she whispered, enticing him closer, wanting another of his tumultuous kisses.

"Hmm," was the extent of his ability to communicate through anything other than touch.

They kissed with scorching intensity, with an urgency surpassing their first kiss. Her fingers nimbly untied his tie and unfastened his shirt buttons. He complemented her actions by making fast work of her buttons, then he shrugged out of his shirt and tossed it to the end of the bed. Wasting no time, she mimicked his movements until they both were nude.

Aware of how quickly they'd gone from being fully clothed to having their clothes wantonly strewn across the bed and carpet, Danielle felt her cheeks redden. Without clothing all the flaws were naked to his discerning eyes. Doubts shrouded her mind. Could he see the tiny lines that indicated she'd lost weight? Did he think her thighs were still a trifle too large for the slimness of her waist? Her breasts were small, too. Did he prefer busty women? Her slender body wasn't perfect; it never had been.

Unaware that she'd also momentarily halted the sweeping motion of her hands going up and down the hollow of his back, she was surprised when George flung himself backward.

He shielded his eyes with his forearm. "I'm not a rutting stallion, Dani. You don't have to freeze up. I can stop whenever you want me to stop."

"I don't think *I* can," she admitted honestly, knowing his stopping was the last thing she wanted to happen. Realizing how he'd misunderstood her momentary hesitation she added, "I guess I'm still self-conscious about getting undressed in front of anyone."

"That's hard to believe. You're incredibly beautiful. I should have told you." He gathered her into his arms, nuzzling the sensitive spot he'd found earlier. "I'm thinking what I should be saying, but my silver tongue is stuck to the roof of my mouth. You blow my mind, sweetheart."

His silence had been the highest form of compliment he could pay her, she realized, both delighted and amazed. "Love me, Giorgio?"

Slowly he lowered his arm and opened his eyes. He did love her. More than physically. Unbeknown to either of them, he must have loved her from afar. Certain she'd reject any declaration of love, that she'd consider it an insincere comment to assure their lovemaking wouldn't end, he bit the side of his cheek to keep from blurting his secret. He needed time to adjust to the insight. Later he'd tell her, he promised. Much, much later, when they were both thinking straight.

He pulled her across his chest, silently loving her with a depth that shocked him.

Danielle splayed her fingers on his chest. The texture of his dark chest hairs contrasted with the sleekness of skin covering his shoulders. Eyes closed, she tactilely memorized each nuance of his masculine torso. But nothing compared to the sensation of his chest against hers.

His hands stroked her, measuring the length of the stroke with her rate of breathing. Alternating deep massaging strokes with a touch as soft and feathery as an ostrich plume, he teased and tormented until Danielle felt a low, hollow, empty feeling in the pit of her stomach. She craved him.

Instinctively, her knees clenched to ease the ache. His fingers caressed her insistently. Of their own accord, her legs parted, allowing him easy access. Waves of pleasure coursed through her.

George wanted to thrust into her immediately. He began counting to fifty by ones, trying to mentally counter his sense of urgency. Hearing her husky whisper of his name had him counting by fives, then tens. He was too hungry for her to delay.

She gasped his name as he entered her. Her appetite for him had gone beyond appetizers.

She wanted all of him. A glorious, pulsating sensation curled low in her stomach.

Her hips arched against him in a rhythm as old as time, but without the boundaries of time. Like her love for him, it could have begun minutes, hours, or decades before. Danielle struggled to take him to the ultimate peak of happiness with the same dedication and stubbornness she'd fought him when they were younger.

Bright, spiraling balls of pure color exploded behind his eyelids as George felt her nails dig into his firm buttocks, felt the small convulsive spasms holding him deep inside of her. He shuddered, giving himself to her with a joy he'd never experienced. In a moment of blinding insight, he knew the difference between lust and love. Lust was bread and water compared to the banquet of emotions and sensations he felt with Danielle.

Danielle held him tightly, reluctant to let go of him. "Stay," she begged without shame.

"Sweetheart . . ." Fearful his weight was crushing her, he shifted both of them to their sides. He wanted to voice the immense satisfaction he felt, but there weren't any words vivid enough to express his feelings. "Ah, sweetheart."

His endearment brought a contented smile to her lips. She knew his near speechlessness was a silent accolade to what they'd shared. Her breathing slowed; her heartbeat returned to normal, but Danielle realized she'd never be the same.

That she'd actually considered substituting a lifetime of platonic friendship for what she'd experienced with George had to be the height of idiocy. Behind his back she twisted the friendship ring on her finger and considered wishing that this night would never end. Silently, she chuckled. Even a magical ring couldn't prevent the sun from rising.

George traced her smile with the tip of his forefinger. "What are you cooking up?"

"Nothing," came her soft whisper as she pulled her arm from beneath him.

"I know better. Tell me what you were thinking," he probed, certain he deserved an answer.

"Silly things."

"For instance?"

"Oh . . . I was just thinking how foolish I've been."

"How?" he asked, his shoulders tensing. He truly would strangle her if she told him she'd just made the biggest mistake of her life. Justifiable homicide. There wouldn't be a male jury in the country that would convict him.

Danielle brushed her fingers across the deep scowl lines on his forehead. "I was thinking about platonic relationships, friendship."

"Forget it. Yeah, I know. I'm the one who offered to be your colleague." He shook his head. "Friendship? That's different. No. Absolutely, irrevocably . . . no! We're going to be one heck of a lot more than friends."

Unable to stop herself, Danielle chuckled aloud. He hadn't told her that he loved her, but he'd come close. Very close. Her hands framed his face as she rubbed the tip of her nose against his. "I couldn't agree more."

CHAPTER FIVE

George cuddled Danielle spoon-fashion, her curved back fitting snugly against him. An inner alarm buzzed in his head demanding immediate attention. Garavelli's was calling. Business before pleasure had been instilled into his mind at an early age. Fresh pasta noodles and loaves of Italian bread wouldn't magically appear for the Saturday-night rush unless he began the kitchen operations early. Inwardly he groaned, reluctant to leave Danielle.

Three years ago he'd slowly begun to take over the operation of the restaurant. Retirement was out of the question for either of his parents. They'd worked side by side operating the family restaurant and simultaneously raising Giorgio and his three rambunctious brothers. But the long hours required had taken their toll on his father's health. Within the first year that George had relieved his folks from the heavy burden, his father had passed away. Isobella had relinquished the reins of running the kitchen, but she remained the grand matriarch. Each evening she made an appearance. Clothed in black, silver hair piled high on her head, she graciously played the role of hostess. Garavelli's guests looked forward to her stopping by their table to socialize.

Weighing and measuring the advantages of following the fine example his parents had provided, George closed his eyes and daydreamed of a future with Danielle. She would be an asset personally and professionally. Undoubtedly, having studied with Charles Du Bois, she could add delectable items to expand the menu. After all, Italian cuisine was the mother of French cooking.

Maybe, he mused, Danielle would regain the weight she'd lost. Fashion be damned, his taste ran toward a curvaceous woman. Danielle had had a perfect figure in high school. Perhaps a little cenci alla fiorentina—deep-fried sweet pastry—would round her figure more to his liking?

Reminded of the pastries that needed to be prepared, he lifted his head from the pillow. He couldn't bring himself to awaken Danielle, but he couldn't refrain from lightly kissing her hand. He raised her left hand. Lazily her fingers naturally curved around his thumb.

Silently, he contemplated leaving a romantic note pinned to his pillow. A simple "I love you" and his signature, he decided. She'd have the majority of the day to think about how she felt toward him.

His lips whispered the message across her knuckles. Her ring scratched the side of his nose. Lifting his head, his eyes widened.

An engagement ring?

He couldn't believe it. Danielle wasn't the type of woman who slept with one man while being engaged to another. Or was she? She'd lived in New York and traveled abroad with Charles Du Bois. Charles was ancient! She couldn't be emotionally involved with him. Or could she?

Latin lovers were notoriously jealous. Giorgio was no exception. Hot-blooded, quick tempered, he struggled to keep from jumping to conclusions.

Danielle marrying an old man and having a young lover on the side left a foul taste in his mouth. The idea of being her *cicisbeo*, gigolo, rubbed him the wrong way. What happened during the night was more than a romantic romp, a one-night stand. He sure as hell wasn't going to allow her to marry a man twice her age!

His breath fanned the tendrils of hair beside her temple. Sorely tempted to conduct an early-morning inquisition, he let fate make his decision by dropping her hand. If she awakened, he'd ask questions. If she didn't, he'd question her later.

Danielle smiled, wriggled her bottom

against him, and slipped the hand bearing the odious ring beneath her pillow.

At least she had the good grace not to snore, he thought, damning the fates as he contemplated stomping around the room to awaken her. His Old World sense of chivalry balked. He'd been taught to be considerate of those he loved. Deciding to let her sleep, he slowly edged off the bed.

He forced himself to dress quietly. His dark, troubled eyes watched her sleeping form, hoping she'd awaken and remove the doubts his keen imagination built. By noon, he knew his temper would be hotter than boiling water.

After he'd dressed, he opened the desk drawer and removed a sheet of hotel stationery and a pen.

He purposely forgot the love note he'd planned on penning and wrote, "Call me at Garavelli's."

Hours later, Danielle reached for him. Her hand patted the pillow where his head should have been. Hesitant to open her eyes and find that she'd been having a gloriously erotic dream, she pulled his pillow against her chest. She detected the faint fragrance of shampoo. She smiled. Her rum and egg shampoo smelled differently. She barely lifted her eyelids, slanting her sleepy eyes from one side of the empty room to the other. Ears attuned for any sound coming from the bathroom, she glanced at her watch.

"Ten fifteen?" she gasped in disbelief, tapping the crystal.

Sleeping late was a habit she despised and seldom did. She considered sleeping past seven in the morning a waste of productive time. She flung the bedcovers aside, bound from the bed, and strode into the bathroom.

Not only had she missed giving George a morning kiss, she'd promised Ellie that she'd be at home in time for coffee and doughnuts. The pastry she didn't need and wouldn't miss, but coffee was another matter. Her eyeballs refused to function properly until she'd had a jolt of caffeine. Hastily she completed her morning ritual and ordered a pot of coffee from room service. She wanted to call her parents, but their phone had been disconnected.

While she was dressing in tobacco-colored trousers and smartly styled elongated silk blouse, she saw the note George had left on the desk. Although totally disconcerted by losing the morning hours, as she'd showered she'd made a mental note to call him once she'd finished sorting through the mementos at her parents. Her first smile of the day faded as she read the brief note.

"What did you expect? A flowery poem?" she chided aloud.

She swallowed a lump of disappointment and considered having room service add a Danish pastry to satisfy her sweet tooth. Deciding she'd be the size of the Goodyear blimp if she let every minor setback trigger her appetite, she paced the floor and waited for her coffee.

George must have been running late, too, she thought, excusing his curt note. Familiar with the hectic pace of a restaurateur, she couldn't blame him for not taking time to write a lengthy letter. After all, it wasn't as though she was returning to New York City that day. She'd call him; they'd make arrangements to—

A sharp rap on her door signaled the arrival of room service. She ushered the young man into her room, had him place the tray on the dresser, tipped him, and ignored the flirtatious wink he gave her as he closed the door.

"College kids," she said, somewhat flattered, somewhat surprised. Her self-perception remained outdated. A college kid didn't wink at someone who outweighed him by ten or fifteen pounds.

She poured a cup, inhaling the aroma appreciatively. Her fingers lingered over the cream pitcher and sugar bowl. Nope, she wouldn't give in to her tendency to feed her frustrations. She couldn't be with George. She'd do the next best thing: talk to him on the telephone.

After obtaining the telephone number, she tried to relax as she waited for him to come to the phone.

"Garavelli's Restaurant" came through the receiver in a pleasant tone of a prerecorded message. Disgusted, Danielle banged the phone down. It would be pointless to leave a message. Within minutes she'd be leaving the hotel and she couldn't be reached at her parents'.

"I need a pick-me-upper," she justified, ripping the corner off three packets of sugar and pouring the white crystals into her coffee. A dribble of cream later, she gulped the coffee.

Self-recrimination being a waste of energy, she banged the cup into its saucer, poured herself another cup and dialed Charles's number.

"Hi, Charles. It's me," she said upon hearing his familiar French accent.

"Danielle! I was just thinking of you, *ma petite*. Are you using your ring to wish yourself back in New York?"

The wistfulness in his voice was easily discernible. He missed her. Knowing she'd barely given him more than a fleeting thought, she coughed to allow time to think of a reply.

"You aren't coming down with a cold, are you?"

"No. My coffee must have gone down the wrong way," she prevaricated, glad he'd been distracted from his original question. "My parents went out last night, so I haven't had a chance to sort through the boxes of mementos yet."

"Poor darling," Charles sympathized.

"First night in your hometown and you had to spend it alone in your hotel room."

The sip of brew she'd taken sputtered in her mouth. She hadn't thought about what she was going to tell Charles. He'd have a heart attack if she blurted out the truth.

"I wasn't alone . . ." She started to gently tell him about George, leaving out the particulars of where he'd spent the night, but when she heard a deep sigh coming across the line, she said, "I ate dinner with Buffy and her new fiancé."

"Buffy is engaged? How wonderful," Charles said. "Good thing you had your ring, otherwise you'd have been a step behind your best friend."

"About the ring, Charles, I told my parents the truth."

Charles laughed. *"Chérie,* the ring entitles you to tell one whopper for each burger you ate during your childhood."

"I couldn't lie to my parents—or anyone else for that matter. I told them it's a friendship ring." She examined the ring, silently appraising it as she spoke. The fake diamond glittered brilliantly in the morning sunlight. "It isn't as though you gave me a real diamond."

"What if I told you the stone is real?"

It was Danielle's turn to laugh. "You'd have to put a mortgage on the family's French château for anything this size."

"Old families have heirlooms."

"This sized heirloom gets stored in a bank vault," she replied, searching the depth of the stone for flaws. She'd read that cubic zirconias were without flaw; diamonds this size usually had visible flaws, unless . . . "Charles, tell me it's costume jewelry so I won't have to rush downstairs and have the desk clerk put it in the vault for safekeeping."

"It's a fake."

His voice mimicked her tones. He'd said exactly what she'd told him to say, but without being able to look him in the eye, she wasn't certain whether she heard the truth or not. "Charles, I want the truth."

"Ah, the truth is what you're seeking. The truth lies in how one perceives what's in front of them. For instance, the rest of the world views you as a sleek, sophisticated woman, but you see yourself as a roly-poly puppy. I've told you how beautiful you are, but you don't believe me. You're having the same problem with the ring. I tell you it's a fake, but because I placed it on your fourth finger where a woman wears an engagement ring, you've begun to wonder . . . is it a wish ring or the real thing?"

Exasperated by his long-winded analogy, Danielle tightened her grip on the receiver. "Yes or no."

"Yes . . . *and* no."

His chuckles were maddening. "Charles, I was out late last night, I should have been at my parents' hours ago, and I don't have time for mind games. Give me a straight answer. Is this stone real or fake?"

"Have you made any wishes on it?"

Danielle felt a rising tide of pink sweeping over her cheeks. "Yes," she admitted without giving details.

"Did they come true?"

Pink changed to beet red. Charles's intuitiveness didn't require explicitness. "Yes."

"Then, my pet, the ring must be real, since it works."

Danielle closed her eyes and pictured him tossing his head back as he laughed. His blue eyes would be twinkling with mischief as he made racy assumptions based on the clues she'd given him.

"You're a clever devil who twists reality until it resembles a fairy tale!" A little clever kink of her own would get a straight story. She crooned sweetly into the phone, "Then we must be engaged, huh?"

Charles's laughter died. He cleared his throat with a mighty hurrumphing noise. Beneath the debonair exterior, he was a practical man. "Can you picture what marriage to a doddering old gentleman such as myself would be like?"

She couldn't, not after last night with George. In fact, she'd never really considered the physical aspects of sharing a bedroom with Charles. In her whimsical mind, she thought they'd continue as before. A change in her last name was all she had imagined.

Diplomatically, she replied, "The right woman would consider herself lucky to be married to you."

"Hmm." His keen ears were sensitive to every inflection in her voice. Something had changed. Taking a wild stab in the dark, he asked, "Did you happen to run across George while you were out?"

"Is that a literal or figurative question?" she returned, grinning.

"Both. Any encounter between the two of you would probably leave George looking at the front of his shirt for tire tracks."

"George made the foursome at Buffy's announcement party. Pure coincidence."

"Providence, thy name is fate," Charles muttered, his tone prosaic. Danielle and George had crossed swords too often for there not to have been an underlying attraction.

"Come on, Charles. You know I don't believe in predestination or fate. Our environment influences where we go, but we take the footsteps that lead to our destiny."

Charles grinned and shook his head. He'd learned from experience that there were certain things in life a man couldn't change. Wisdom, knowing when to fight and knowing when to accept defeat, came with age. Youth was wasted on the young. George and Danielle were meant for each other, regardless of how they fought each other and the fates. He'd have to regard the time she'd been with him as a bonus gift from the gods for his leading a virtuous life.

"Pure coincidence," he repeated, then added, "You'll be seeing George again?"

"I'm supposed to call him at work."

"Did you happen to mention my offer to financially back you if you decided to open a restaurant in Williamsburg?"

"Vaguely. Buffy and Mario arrived before I could fully explain what you have in mind."

"George wouldn't object to competition?"

"Different customers. Garavelli's is a homey place. Your ideas are strictly linen tablecloth and crystal."

"*Our* ideas," he corrected selfishly, unable to stop himself from voicing the disparaging differences in style. Love was one thing, but Danielle wasting her culinary talents on making pizza horrified him. "You've got to run. Give Ellie a kiss on each cheek for me."

"Will do."

"Call and let me know when to pick you up at the airport. 'Bye."

" 'Bye."

Danielle returned the receiver to its cradle. The glittering stone winked at her. Charles had a knack of muddling her mind to make her see with clarity. She refused to worry about the value of the ring, being more concerned with Charles's reaction to knowing she'd gone out with George. From the undertones of the conversation, Charles had deduced her change of heart and wasn't the

98

least bit upset. They'd continue to be the best of friends.

She picked up her purse and a light jacket that matched her trousers and crossed to the door. She'd try to contact George after she returned to the hotel. By then, she reasoned, he'd be finished with the lunch hour business and the recorder wouldn't be on the telephone.

Danielle parked the rental car beside her father's silver Mercedes. A peculiar lump rose in her throat as she glanced at the home she'd been raised in. Although Ellie had planted a border of fall mums that were in full bloom, the two-storied frame house appeared desolate without the ruffled white curtains hanging in the windows. The for-sale sign had SOLD stickered across the front. She hadn't lived there for years, but she'd always think of it as home.

Before she could climb the porch steps she heard "She's here! See, I told you she'd be here in time for lunch" coming from inside.

"Dani!" Her father hugged her as she crossed the threshold. "Your mother has been henpecking me to drive over to the hotel. I told her—" He shrugged and smiled. "You'd think after forty years I'd quit trying to tell her anything, wouldn't you?"

"Hi, sweetheart," Ellie greeted, giving her daughter a quick hug and her husband a dirty look. "I heard those remarks. If it weren't for me, your father wouldn't have gone out for hamburgers. He'd let you starve."

"Bicker, bicker, bicker," Danielle chided, suddenly ravenous for the hamburger, French fries, and creamy chocolate milkshake that awaited her in the kitchen. Oral gratification, her reward for listening to parental discord.

"How's Buffy?" Dan asked. He looped his arm across her shoulders and ushered her into the dinette area.

"Fine. She and Mario Garavelli announced their engagement last night."

"Buffy? Engaged?"

A stricken glance passed between her parents that Danielle ignored. She helped Ellie unpack the food and replied succinctly, "Yep."

"Last night your mother and I discussed Charles giving you a friendship ring," her father said, bouncing from one point to the next without a pause. He slowly unwrapped his burger. "Believe it or not, we finally agreed on something."

"What's that?"

"We want grandchildren," Ellie stated in a flat, matter-of-fact voice.

Danielle bit into her burger. Good manners gave her the excuse she needed to keep her mouth shut while chewing her food. She supposed that wanting grandchildren was a natural state of affairs. Obviously, from the supportive looks passing between them, they'd decided that perpetuation of the Brewster genes was a solid reason for disliking the idea of her marrying Charles.

Smiling inwardly, but wrinkling her brow in a thoughtful frown, she wondered where she got the audacity to ask, "Is it too late for the two of you to consider having another child? I've always wanted a brother or sister."

Danielle lifted one shoulder and cocked her head to one side, giving the impression of being all ears, waiting for a response.

Her father grinned; her mother glared.

"Oh well, just a thought." Danielle submerged a French fry in catsup. Discussing sex, or making babies as her mother called it, was strictly taboo—especially at the lunch table. Knowing perfectly well her mother had depended on the school system to inform her one and only child about sex education, she asked, "I didn't offend you, did I?"

"I declare," her mother gasped, scraping her chair back from the table. "I never thought I'd live to see the day that—"

Dan interrupted the beginning of Ellie's familiar tirade by chuckling. "We asked for that, Ellie. Our daughter isn't a teenager."

"She's still our daughter," Ellie huffed, hands on her hips.

"We questioned her about a private matter. Is it unfair for her to turn the tables, so to speak?"

Danielle winked a silent thanks to her dad as the front doorbell rang.

"That's Buffy. I invited her over to go through the snapshots with me. Do you mind?" Danielle scooted her chair away from the table. Her friend's arrival couldn't have been more timely. "Excuse me."

She ran to the door, flinging it wide open, glad to be off the hot seat in the kitchen. "Hi . . ." her voice rose abruptly when she saw who was attached to the finger pressing the doorbell. "George?"

Without so much as a greeting he asked, "Whose ring is that on your finger?"

Danielle grinned. Charles, she mused, would love the stink he had caused by giving her this bauble. She stepped out on the porch, out of hearing range for her parents. "Mine. It was a gift."

Taking her hand, George pulled Danielle down the steps, toward his car. "You love tormenting me, don't you?"

"Keeps the adrenaline moving. It's lunchtime. Why aren't you at Garavelli's?"

"Don't sidetrack me." Although he gave the appearance of being irate, the moment she'd stepped outside and he'd taken her hand, he'd realized how ridiculous he was being to charge over to her parents' house and demand answers. George was perfectly capable of laughing at his bizarre behavior. His dark eyes lit with amusement. He swung around, drawing her into his arms. "On second thought, want to go find an isolated dirt road out in the country?"

His fast shift caught Danielle off guard. Or was it the glitter in his eyes? Or the beguiling tilt of his lips? An overwhelming desire to reach up, grab him, and kiss him made her heart pound faster. From the look in his eyes he was thinking similar thoughts.

"That's a difficult offer to refuse." She tossed her head toward the windows behind her. "Do we have an audience?"

"One parent at each window." He cradled her closer. Her eyes latched onto his lips as they inched lower. "Want to give them something to talk about?"

She didn't have to look over her shoulder to know their reaction. Her father would grin from ear to ear while he applauded. Her mother would be pleasantly appalled at the public display of affection. Both of them would quit worrying about Charles being unable to produce the grandchildren. George Garavelli would be welcomed with open arms.

But she wasn't going to kiss George to please her parents—only herself.

Reflexively, she raised on tiptoe. Her arms crept up the front of his shirt of their own accord. Lips parted, she offered a silent affirmative reply.

CHAPTER SIX

"Yoo-hoo!" Ellie shouted from the front stoop. "Danielle, invite George to come in."

Danielle groaned for George's benefit. "I'll apologize now."

Good-naturedly, George brushed a kiss on her forehead. "Your mother can't be any worse than mine."

"Humph! You don't know what took place before you arrived. If my furniture weren't en route to Florida I'd have been sent to bed without lunch."

George frowned. His hand settled below her waist where he could feel her protruding hip bone. "You can't afford to skip any meals."

As she climbed the steps, she wondered if his remark was a backhanded compliment or an insult. She refrained from asking when she spied Dan and Ellie standing inside the storm door with their noses pressed against the glass panes.

George grinned. Danielle's parents must be hassling her with the same questions he received on a daily basis. When are you going to settle down with a good woman? Why haven't you married? Where are my grandchildren?

This morning, while he'd been helping in the kitchen he'd finally found the elusive answer: Danielle Brewster. He'd left the restaurant in the middle of the lunch rush to tell her that he loved her. Ring or no ring, she wasn't going past the city limits without him.

His off-centered smile broadened as he thought of an appropriate way to spike her parents' guns and circumvent any protests from Danielle. Mario had the right idea. Avoid rejection by consulting the woman's parents first. Danielle might kill him later, he thought, but he was willing to take the risk.

"Dan. Ellie. I hope you don't mind my dropping by unannounced," George said as he shook Dan's hand. "I need to talk to you."

"About the party tomorrow?" Ellie inquired. Beaming her approval toward Danielle, she led the way toward the only room with furniture, the dinette area.

"No." George turned toward Dan. "Sir, would you object to my marrying your daughter?"

Danielle felt her knees buckle. She plopped into the chair George held for her. "Uh, George . . . could we—"

"I'd be proud to call you son," her father replied, pounding George on the shoulders.

Ellie clapped her hands with delight. "Oh, Dani, you should have told us. You're such a little scamp."

"But, Mother, Dad . . ." Helplessly her hands fluttered from one parent to the next, then toward George. Three smug smiles met her baffled expression. Conspirators! Her first impulse was to grab her burger, inhale it, and then hustle George outside. On second thought, she pasted a wide smile on her lips and said, "George, dear, don't we have something to discuss—immediately?"

"Of course not." Ellie wasn't going to let anyone get a cross word in to spoil Danielle's chances for marrying Williamsburg's most eligible bachelor. "George is supposed to ask your father first, then you. Etiquette, you know. Sit down, George. Join us for lunch. Dan, you did get extra burgers, didn't you?" She reached into the sack. "Here's one. I'd warm it in the microwave, but heating mayonnaise isn't a good idea. Fries?"

"Mother, stop it." She shot George a silent appeal to tell them he was joking.

Shaking his head, George accepted the hamburger. "Thanks. Would you object to us announcing our engagement at your party?"

"No!" Danielle objected. She had no intention of letting anyone ramrod her into marriage. Not her parents, not George, not anybody!

George patted her hand. "I asked your parents. We'll discuss the other niceties later." He grinned when her toe jammed against his shin.

"No, we don't object," Dan replied, speaking for himself and Ellie. "Perhaps we should increase the order of champagne, though. Sounds as if we have lots to celebrate."

"Dad, you've agreed to let George ask me to marry him. I haven't accepted."

Her father had always helped her out of tight spots. He couldn't miss the direct appeal she was making to stop this farce. Dan refused to meet her eyes. She knew what he was going to say before he opened his mouth.

"Dani, your fiancé asking permission was a courteous formality. In today's day and age, I'm certain you've given him some reason to believe you would accept his proposal."

George opened his mouth, then wisely closed it when she kicked his shin for the second time. Her father could talk about "this day and age," but she knew he was decidedly old-fashioned. She could graciously keep silent, or blab and have her father oiling up the shotgun. Either way, the end result was the same.

Of all the dirty tricks she'd played on George Garavelli, he'd topped every one of them in one fell blow. Revenge? Hadn't Buffy warned her about paying for any previous slight she'd given George? The scoundrel could get final revenge by jilting her five minutes after the announcement was made at the party.

She'd be humiliated. Devastated. Her parents' party would be ruined. Yes, if George Garavelli wanted revenge, he'd have it. What she had to do was think of a way to avert the disaster.

Her mind raced a mile a minute while George, Dan, and Ellie discussed the specifics of making the announcement.

The left side of her brain calculated a maneuver to extricate her from George's wily plot, but the right side of her brain pricked holes in her basic premise. What made her think George wanted revenge? He'd forgotten his reason for storming over here the moment he saw her. He'd kissed her. That didn't sound like a man who was intent on getting revenge. That sounded more like a man who really wanted to marry her.

Then why didn't he consult her before asking for her hand in marriage? came from the left. He wanted revenge!

Nonsense! the right side argued. He was bold and brash. Love made a man do extraordinary things. Her parents' departure was imminent, as was hers. He had to do something drastic.

Love? He had never even spoken the word.

It was implied, her conscience countered.

The left side cackled at the right side's naïveté. Lust, not love, motivated Giorgio. That was no basis for a marriage. She'd be better off with Charles.

Don't be so damned practical, the right side argued. Charles was her friend. She loved George.

She'd be smart to tell George that Charles's

ring was the real thing. She couldn't marry him because she was engaged to good old reliable Charles.

She didn't lie to anyone, not even herself.

While the two halves of Danielle's brain waged war on each other, George kept a wary eye on her as he listened to Dan and Ellie make honeymoon suggestions. Ellie favored Florida; Dan recommended New York City. George felt certain his recalcitrant fiancée was making plans of her own that didn't include him.

The moment she'd lapsed into silence and quit kicking his shins, he should have carried her off in his arms to the nearest bed. Better yet, he mused, to the nearest justice of the peace. He didn't want her thinking . . . only feeling.

He watched her eyes narrow and he inwardly cringed, fully aware that silence did not mean consent. Danielle Brewster wasn't a woman who allowed herself to be pushed around by any man. He'd learned that lesson when he'd tried to bully her into putting her name opposite his on the election ballot. She'd campaigned against him, but she hadn't defeated him then and he wouldn't allow her to defeat him now.

"I'll get that," Danielle said when she heard the doorbell ring. It was apparent to her that they didn't need her around to make plans. "Better be careful, George. I think they're wangling you into doubling on your honeymoon."

George shifted in his chair, but managed a wan smile. "What do you think of New Orleans, sweetheart?"

"You decide," she replied pointedly. She hadn't been in on any previous decisions. Why did he think she'd agree on a place to honeymoon? Hell's bells, she hadn't agreed to marrying him.

Standing, George excused himself and followed her into the hallway. Bold as brass he whispered, "You can thank me now."

Stunned, she wheeled around. "Thank you? For what? Your incredible nerve?"

"Cast iron stomach," he concurred, but sticking his hand forward he made it tremble. "But my nerves are shot. Asking for a woman's hand in marriage is tough work. Dangerous, too. One more swift kick and I'd have been crippled for life."

"I should have aimed higher. That would have ended the honeymoon prattle."

George shot her a roguish grin. "You should be thanking me. Didn't I save you from being sent to bed without dinner?"

"Some things are worse than skipping a meal, George Garavelli," she hissed. "I feel sorry for the woman you do marry."

"Don't feel sorry for yourself," he teased, skirting around her to open the door. "Self-pity is a bad habit to get into."

Raising her fists toward the ceiling, she

ground her back molars at his temerity. He'd regret putting her in an untenable situation. By God, it would serve him right if she married him to get even for his audacious treatment.

"It would serve you right if I did marry you. I could make your life miserable."

"That's a chance I'll have to take, isn't it?"

"You're impossible!"

"So are you," he replied, unruffled. "How about a good-bye kiss to tide me over until later?" He caught her hand as she shook her fist under his nose. Courageously he lifted her knuckles to his lips. "No good-bye kiss for your fiancé? What's everyone going to think?"

"Don't you dare tell anyone else. It's bad enough that you've told my parents this cock and bull story. They may never speak to you again."

"Hmm. I'll wager that you're the one they aren't speaking to," he taunted, loving how her eyes sparkled and her face had colored a rosy pink. "They think I'm God's gift to their spinster daughter."

"Why you egotistical maniac!" Pushed beyond measure, she waved her fourth finger bearing the fake ring in his face. "You aren't the only man who's interested in me."

"Maybe not, but I'm the man you're going to marry. We're perfect for each other. Admit it."

His thumb made persuasive playful circles

on her inner wrist while his dark eyes made erotic promises no healthy female could ignore. The circumspect kiss they'd shared in the front yard had left her wanting. She felt her anger deflate as though she were a half-baked cake and the oven door had been slammed.

Seeing her weaken, George pushed his advantage by kissing the corner of her mouth on one side, then the other. Her bottom lip trembled in expectation.

Oh no, sweet love, he mused, he was going to leave her hungering for more.

He reached behind his back and opened the door. "Be ready."

Standing on the front steps, Buffy heard George and saw the dreamy, addlepated look on Danielle's face. "George? What are you doing here?" she demanded.

"Saying good-bye to my fiancée." He curved his finger under Buffy's chin and closed her gaping mouth. He'd suspected at one point that she had a crush on him, but her loyalty to Danielle kept her from doing anything other than placing orders for take-out pizza at Garavelli's. "Looks as though you and I are going to be cousins-in-law."

"Kissing cousins?" Buffy squeaked, in a state of shock.

George shook his head and glanced over his shoulder. "Danielle is stingy with my kisses. She wants all or nothing."

"I'm in love with Mario," Buffy reminded herself aloud. "I can't kiss you."

Danielle pulled Buffy into the hallway to get her out of George's proximity. The last person she'd allow him to kiss was her best friend, especially since Buffy had shared some particularly lurid fantasies regarding kissing George Garavelli. If George was set on revenge, she wasn't going to stand by and let it affect Buffy's future.

Giving George a casual wave, Danielle followed Buffy up the steps leading to her bedroom. "Mom, Buffy's here. We're going to sort through the boxes. Are they in my room?"

"Yes, dear." Ellie scurried from the kitchen to the curved bannister at the foot of the steps. "Just think, you and Buffy are both going to have the same last names—like sisters."

Danielle realized her mother wasn't fooled by the silent treatment she'd given them at the table. Ellie was going to use every advantage she could think of to get her daughter married to George Garavelli.

"Sisters?" Buffy whispered in awe. "I used to pretend we were sisters."

"Pull up a piece of the floor and sit down before you fall down," Danielle offered, crossing her legs and sitting Indian-style beside a large box.

"Up until last night you hated George. Are you really going to marry Garlic Mouth?"

Grinning, knowing her friend was in shock

and completely confused, Danielle said, "He asked my parents, not me."

"He asked your parents to marry him? Is that legal?"

Danielle rolled backward, laughing as she folded her hands behind her head. Her best buddy was one of those special people who had an intelligence quota over two hundred, but a common-sense factor of minus ten. "George did what Mario did last night."

"Now I am confused." Buffy held her temples as though she were caught in a time warp and the room were spinning out of control. "Mario asked your parents to marry him, too? Does that mean he isn't going to marry me?"

"You are dazed, silly. Like Mario, George asked my father for my hand in marriage *before* he asked me to marry him. What do you think?"

"I think I must be drunk. Sharing a glass of red wine at lunch with Mario is pretty heady stuff."

"No, Buffy." She slowly paced her words. "What do you think of George wanting to marry me?"

"I think one of us is crazy as a bedbug. Are you in some kind of trouble?"

"No, why?"

"There has to be some plausible reason for you marrying your life-long enemy. Did you and Charles have a fight?"

"Nope." She held the ring up. "He gave me a wish ring before I left."

Buffy took one look at the huge diamond and fell backward. "That's a diamond?"

"Yes and no."

"A yes-and-no diamond," Buffy repeated, one side of her mouth tugged askew. "That makes as much sense as anything else I've heard since arriving here. Why do I feel as though I'm at the Mad Hatter's tea party without an invitation?"

"It's crazy all right," Danielle agreed. She shoved a box between them and dipped into its contents. "Here, you look through these."

"Dani, are you going to accept George's proposal?" Buffy began sorting the pictures into two piles. One stack was family pictures, the other of Danielle and her friends. "It would be wonderful to have you back in Virginia."

"Charles and I talked about opening a restaurant here," she replied, avoiding a direct response to the initial question. "I don't have to marry anyone to change where I live."

"Something tells me that George is going to veto that idea." She held a photo up for Danielle's inspection. "Halloween."

"Aargh! That tutu makes me look like a hippo."

"I thought you looked like a real ballerina. I hated the happy witch costume my mother made. Is this a keeper?"

"Set it aside for my parents. Hey, look at this." Danielle pointed to a picture she'd taken at a high-school basketball game. "I loved Coach Kent."

"You never told me you had a crush on him." Buffy's blue eyes widened in surprise. "I thought we shared our deepest, darkest secrets."

Danielle giggled. "I loved Coach because he kept George warming the bench during the basketball season. Look at George. He's chafing at the bit to get out on the court."

"Considering George was eight inches shorter than the smallest player, I don't think you had much cause to gloat."

"Remember how we cut out printed words from magazines and gave the pictures captions? I'd name this one Cut Down to Size."

"Too Short to Slam-Dunk is more accurate. What about this one?" She held a picture of George and the captain of the cheerleading squad toward Danielle. "Why'd you take it?"

"Don't you remember her?"

"Rita? Sure. She was the first one in our class to get married after graduation."

"Yeah. When I took this, she was on the ballot for class president—running against George."

"You campaigned for her. She lost?"

"Lost? Ha! The minute she thought George was going to invite her to the prom she quit campaigning. She could have won if she'd tried."

Buffy closely examined the svelte glamour

queen of their class. "Didn't George take his next-door neighbor?"

"Hmm. She outweighed me by ten pounds, but everybody liked her."

"You said that as though you weren't popular." Buffy thumped her flat chest. "I was the class nerd."

"You weren't."

"You didn't see me that way, but everybody else thought I was too tall, too scrawny, with dishwater blond hair, four eyes, and braces."

"You were voted Sweetest Girl our senior year." Danielle dug to the bottom of the box for the yearbook. She hastily flipped through the pages to prove her point. "See!"

"So who wants to be sweet? I wanted to be sexy. Remember my motto? 'What God's forgotten I'll stuff with cotton'?" She threw her shoulders back. "Talk about mixed up. One day I'd be a 40D sweater girl, and the next day a 32A in a prim white blouse."

Laughing, Danielle reached over and ruffled her friend's tawny blond hair. With her porcelain skin and great bone structure, Buffy could have gone to New York and been a successful model. Aside from her high cheekbones, she had gorgeous slender legs that seemed to start at her neck and go on forever. Over the years, her gawky, coltish walk had changed to a loose-limbed, graceful stride.

"I know New York models who'd kill not to have to worry about their weight."

Buffy giggled. "Remember that awful jock who called us the Lost and Found Twins?"

"Uh-huh. He said you'd lose weight and I'd find it. At least you didn't have to go to Omar the Tentmaker to get your graduation gown."

"Now who's exaggerating?" Buffy turned the page. "You were voted Girl Most Likely to Succeed."

Staring at the picture, Danielle grinned. It appeared as though a decapitated head had been placed on a speaker's podium. She had been a master at hiding her plump body. Automatically her hands slid over her trim hips.

"I guess how we see ourselves is indelibly printed in our minds, isn't it?" Danielle said thoughtfully. "I still reach for the size sixteens when I shop."

"Oh yeah? That makes me feel better. I've worn contacts for years, but I catch myself searching for my glasses every now and then." Buffy scrutinized her closest friend. "We changed on the outside, but not the inside?"

Danielle tapped her skull. "Bubble-butt is alive and well up here. When mother called and insisted I fly here, I almost didn't come."

"Oh Dani, Bubble-butt was never a derogatory name."

Raising one eyebrow, Danielle shook her head.

"George called you that, but I overheard him tell the guys on the baseball team that you had the cutest tush in town."

"George said that?"

"Yeah." Buffy leaned forward and whispered. "Don't tell anybody, but after I heard him say that, I bought a pair of those padded panties."

"Why didn't you tell me?"

"You hated him, remember? You'd have spent your allowance on buying girdles. Besides, I had a king-sized crush on him back then."

"Then?" Danielle teased. "I could swear you were tempted to kiss him today."

"I love Mario, but I have to admit, there is a strong family resemblance in the Garavelli family." Buffy gave Dani a mischievous grin. "I can't wait for Isobella to corner you."

"Parents," Dani sighed in the same tone she'd used as a teenager. "Dad and Mom are thrilled with the idea of having George as a son-in-law. They had a conniption fit when they thought Charles had given me an engagement ring. All of a sudden they've decided they want to be grandparents."

"Aha!" Buffy dropped the yearbook and grabbed Dani's hand. "It is real."

"It's not an engagement ring, if that's what you're thinking. I took it believing it was a cubic zirconia."

Buffy moved her hand beside Danielle's. Her diamond, a full carat, looked small in comparison. "Charles is rich, isn't he?"

She could answer a million and one questions about Charles, right down to his favorite brand of Russian paprika, but they had never discussed his financial status. He lived in the same apartment building where she lived. He dressed impeccably. Never a silver hair out of place or too long, never a hangnail on his slender fingers, never a day without cut flowers in his apartment. She suspected his family was wealthy, but that didn't mean Charles was rolling in dough.

"Charles says a man's wealth is measured by the happiness he gives and receives." She imitated his Gallic shrug. "By his standards, he's very wealthy."

"That's no help," Buffy complained. "Why don't we go to a jewelry store and have it appraised?"

Danielle shook her head. "It's a friendship ring. He gave it to me to make me happy."

"I'll bet it doesn't make George happy," Buffy droned. "What are you going to do with two engagement rings? Wear them in tandem?"

"I can't convince myself George intends to marry me." Her chin dropped to her chest. "Last night you thought he wanted revenge. Have you changed your mind?"

"It's possible George saw the ring and . . ." Buffy grimaced. Her mind expanded the premise of revenge to a full-blown hypothesis. "George thinks you're engaged, so he sweeps you off your feet. He requests for your hand in marriage. You give Charles his ring back. George dumps you like yesterday's gummy noodles."

"Point A to point B to point C. I can see why you're a geometry teacher. One, two, three—he gets even." Danielle felt a sharp pain in the region of her heart. "I guess I'm a cock-eyed optimist, but I can't accept the cut-and-dried formula."

"Me, neither. I may teach higher mathematics, but that doesn't mean I have a calculator for a heart. I just don't want to see you hurt. Why don't you sign some sort of prenuptial agreement?"

Danielle grinned at the ridiculous suggestion.

"You wouldn't put batter on a cookie sheet without knowing how long to cook it, would you?"

"Buffy, you can't be serious."

"I am serious. You know, something like . . ." Buffy tapped her finger on her chin thoughtfully. "You both set a wedding date. He defaults; you get to throw meat cleavers at him at ten paces."

"That's being serious?" Danielle giggled. Despite her faultless logic, Buffy had an irrepressible sense of humor. "What if I default?"

Buffy turned her hands palms upward. "It's a woman's prerogative to change her mind."

"You may be his kissing cousin—"

"But I'm your friend." Buffy hugged Danielle. "Will you be my maid of honor?"

Feeling tears scalding her eyes, Danielle

blinked. Eons ago they had planned their weddings from white satin dresses beaded with pearls to the sexy garters they'd wear. "Yes."

"This time next month, I'll be Mrs. Mario Garavelli." Buffy sat back on her heels. "And you'll be Mrs. Giorgio Garavelli."

Danielle smiled dubiously. "Don't count on it, Ms. Math Teacher. Sometimes a straight line isn't the shortest distance between two points."

"Meaning?"

"George took a shortcut when he bypassed asking me."

Picking up another stack of pictures, Buffy grumbled, "He had to skip the preliminaries. You're leaving town Monday."

"Monday," Danielle repeated, remembering how she'd felt when she'd left years before. She'd had mixed emotions then too. Smothered by parental love, and yet she had felt a keen sense of being abandoned—kicked out of the family nest—expected to soar alone. Eager and hesitant. Scared and confident.

She'd survived, more than survived. She'd slimmed down, toned up, and found a new identity. She was no longer Bubble-butt or half of the Lost and Found Twins. She was Danielle Brewster, chef *extraordinaire*.

Yes, Monday she would leave Williamsburg. Her chin raised fractionally. And if Giorgio Garavelli's intentions were less than honorable, if they were based on getting revenge, he'd meet a formidable opponent. Charles, with his infinite wisdom, had been right.

What difference did it make what people had thought of her in the past?

Come Monday, she could board the plane with her head held high—with or without George Garavelli. Be it love or revenge that motivated George, he'd learn that he wasn't the only person in Williamsburg with a recipe for cooked goose.

CHAPTER SEVEN

Long after Danielle and Buffy had finished sorting the mementos and she'd watched her friend gobble down the brownies her mother had brought as a snack, Danielle returned to her hotel room.

Her dark eyes glittered with anticipation as she showered, applied fresh makeup, and dressed. Her dark hair was artfully scooped off her nape, held by combs, and curled until ringlets cascaded loosely from the crown of her head. She'd chosen to wear the cream-colored cashmere dress she'd bought in New York. The high neck, long sleeves, straight skirt, and narrow belt were understated but chic, she decided as she latched the clip on three strands of perfectly matched pearls. White on white—the ultimate in sophisticated wear.

With careful deliberation, she'd over-dressed for the casual family restaurant. She'd dispensed with her wardrobe of sloppy over-sized sweaters and jeans the day she'd pulled on a pair of size ten corduroy trousers without having to lie on the bed to get the zipper up. Her present attire silently alerted anyone who saw her that she'd changed.

"Coming," she called when she heard a sharp rap on the door. She removed the chain latch and opened the door.

Dressed in a black tuxedo with black satin lapels, George stood within inches of her, twirling a single red rose in a crystal vase. His dark devilish looks were a perfect foil for the pristine white shirt and black bow tie. He wore the formal evening clothes as though he'd been born in them.

Danielle felt her resolve to confront him wither like sheets of dried phyllo dough. A hot current flashed through her, curling her toes in her cream satin high-heeled shoes, singeing the ends of her hair. His ability to do the unexpected constantly knocked her off guard.

"Come in," she bade in a voice a bare decibel above a whisper.

When he lowered his head and brushed a kiss on her cheek before accepting her invitation, she found herself wanting to invite him into more than her room. Her hands visibly trembled as she reached for him, taking his gift. "It's beautiful. Thank you."

George felt dumbstruck. With superhuman effort he managed to walk rather than stumble into her room. The second he heard the door-latch click, he knew he'd made a major strategical error. How the hell was he going to get out of there without making love to her?

His dark eyes automatically were drawn to the floral bedspread. Sheer willpower kept him from tossing her on the bed for the second time, but with a totally different intent this time. No anger. Only love.

He wanted to unravel her virginal white dress thread by thread. He wanted to sink himself into her softness with an urgency beyond anything he'd ever felt or was likely to feel with any other woman. He wanted to brand her as being his permanently before taking her to the pinnacle of ecstasy.

Straightening his shoulders, he adopted a casual air and strolled further into the room. "You look gorgeous."

Danielle licked her dry lips as she placed his gift on the triple dresser and rested one hip on the same surface to give her knees a chance to recover. She'd observed the direction his eyes had taken. Lord, if he wanted revenge, she was certainly willing to avail herself.

His black eyes scorched her as they slowly took a second look. The tips of her breasts hardened as though his hands and mouth had touched them. Embarrassed by her easy arousal, knowing the clinging cashmere was revealing the effect he had on her, she plucked the bodice loose as she fiddled with her pearls. His crooked smile warned her that he'd seen the ineffective gesture and knew exactly what she was doing.

"Nervous?" he asked, strangling on his own saliva. He could taste the memory of her breasts on his tongue. Sweet, pert, and responsive lingered on his taste buds.

"I wasn't until you arrived," she blurted with honesty. "Your eyes should be outlawed."

"Come here and close them."

Danielle couldn't move. "How?"

"I kiss with my eyes shut," he whispered with longing. Desire reduced him to begging, "Come kiss me, please."

"Giorgio . . ." Her hand fluttered in a futile gesture as he began to close the space between them.

"Do you know what it does to me when you call me by my given name?"

She blinked. His eyes were burning with such intensity that it hurt to look at them. Her hands raised in mute protest.

Giorgio circled her waist and pulled her up against him. Unashamed that his arousal was as obvious as hers, he rocked her in the cradle of his pelvis. "Yes, sweetheart, feel what you do to me. All I have to do is look at you and hear you speak my name. I haven't thought of anything today but a hundred different ways I want to make love to you."

"Giorgio, we can't. We're expected—"

His lips danced across her cheek to the pearl stud in her earlobe. He sipped, drawing the hard pearl into his mouth. Subconsciously, she knew he'd substituted the pearl for her hardened nipple. A tiny startled sound hissed through her lips when his tongue circled the shell of her ear.

She parted her lips to mindlessly repeat her objection, hanging on to sanity by a slender thread. He took what she wouldn't give, oblivious to anything she said, listening only to the pounding beat of her heart for guidance. In one bold stroke, he thrust inside her sweetness. A low growl of satisfaction came from his chest.

His mouth rocked back and forth, changing the feel of his lips, teeth, and tongue. The tiny serrated edge of his teeth bit the bow of her lip, sensitizing it until it caught fire, burning away her resistance, making her temporarily forget her doubts. Hot, slow, swirling, teasing, caressing, drawing her tongue inside his mouth. She shivered at the intimacy of discovering his unique taste. She began to move her tongue as he had. He deepened each stroke, ravishing her mouth and being ravished in return.

When he lifted his mouth, hers followed, wanting him, trembling with need. The tip of his tongue met hers. Unable to endure another soul kiss, he slowly turned her in his arms until she faced the mirror. His forearm rested beneath her breasts; his other arm wrapped low on her hips.

"I love seeing you like this, feeling you,

knowing I've done this to you. Did you think by covering yourself from head to toe that you'd turn me off? No zipper. No buttons. Were you telling me you're inaccessible? Are you trying to drive me out of my mind?"

"No." Her head lolled against his shoulder. Through her lashes she saw his hand cup her breast, roll her nipple between his thumb and forefinger, lightly pinching it until pleasure came close to pain, then he soothed it with the fleshy pad of his thumb. Below her waist, his fingers splayed, his thumb covering the shallow dimple, his small finger rubbing the lacy edging of her bikini panties. "No, but you're driving me crazy."

He rewarded her honesty with a love-bite on her nape. He loved the lambent glitter of passion in her eyes, the swollen pout of her lips from having been thoroughly kissed. But he'd promised himself that he wouldn't completely make love to her until she'd removed the diamond from her finger. There wasn't room for two men in her life, and he was about to prove that he alone was the man she wanted.

She squirmed against him when his right hand began bunching her dress upward. "Don't."

"Don't touch you? Don't kiss you? Oh, sweetheart, I couldn't stop now if I wanted to —and I don't."

His lips made forays on her neck as his hand boldly stroked the front of her legs and pulled her skirt with its attached satin lining above her panty line. She sucked in her stomach when she felt his hand beneath the satin, touching her hot skin. The dresser pressed into her thighs as she instinctively arched against the palm of his hand.

"Yes. Show me what you want. Don't be afraid," he whispered when he felt her back momentarily stiffen. "I have to know how to love you. See how my hands mold you against me?" His breath feathered the curls beside her ear. His fingers nestled into the dark curls hiding the secret source of her passion. "God, sweetheart, you're melting like hot, sweet candy."

His left hand dipped beneath her hem, pulling her dress high enough to unsnap the front catch of her lacy bra. She heard him groan, felt his hips rotate. Dizzily, she spun as he propelled her around, sweeping her dress over her head.

"This isn't fair," she gasped when she felt his satin lapels against her breasts.

"Shh, love, relax. Let me pleasure you."

His mouth covered hers and his fingers synchronized with his thrusting tongue. She reached for him, but he moved, forestalling access. Frustration laced ecstasy as she felt herself twist against his hand, showing him what felt good. His skillful hands consumed her.

"Giorgio, stop. I'm going to—"

His thumb moved over the tight bud making her shiver with pleasure. "Yes, sweet love, yes. Let go." He whispered encouragement until tiny showers of sparks enveloped her. She was beyond seeing, beyond hearing, she only felt. She tried to speak, but couldn't. She responded with abandonment. She bit her lip to keep from screaming. Only a husky cry of relief indicated the pleasure she'd received.

George slowed his fingers, enjoying her climax as though it were his own. He could slowly build her to a second peak that would be higher, more intense, but his control was slipping. He'd wanted to wrap her legs around his waist and thrust deeply inside the moist slipperiness that he'd created.

Lifting her, he settled her on the bed under the coverlet, then removed his tuxedo as he watched her skim her hands over the places he'd thoroughly caressed. One knee was slightly bent. Innocent. Provocative. Satiated, he mused with a smile.

He'd taken her on a solo flight to heaven, but she still refused to say what he wanted desperately to hear. Three simple words: *I love you.* Maybe not so simple considering their history of open warfare.

During the few hours they'd been separated, with Buffy's help, she had rebuilt her defenses. He'd known it when he saw her at the door. She'd been excruciatingly polite. His smile broadened. She hadn't thanked him for loving her. Had she done so, he would probably have tanned her delectable backside.

There was one barrier keeping him from joining her on the bed. He'd vowed early in life not to fool around with a woman who belonged to another man. Last night he hadn't noticed the ring. Considering the size of that rock, he must have been blind, or subconsciously he'd blocked it from registering in his mind. With that admission, he reaffirmed his determination not to play second cook in any woman's kitchen. He'd wait, regardless of how long it took, for her to remove the ring of her own volition.

Danielle watched Giorgio through fringed eyelashes. Amazed at his self-control and her lack of inhibitions, she wondered what he was thinking. His smile was difficult to read. Triumph? Smugness? Pleasure? Or was he laughing at her for thinking she could resist his considerable charms? Frankly, she didn't know or care.

She stretched lazily, pulled the sheet against her breasts, and sat up in the bed. "What are you waiting for? An invitation?"

"Something like that. I promised myself I wouldn't make love to you until you removed that ring."

"It isn't an engagement ring." Her hand clenched. At the airport she had promised Charles that she'd wear it. Maybe she was being superstitious, but both wishes she'd made had been granted, both wishes had centered around George. What would happen if she took it off? Silently she chastised herself. Wish rings and Aladdin's lamps were fairy-tale stuff. But a promise made to a dear friend wasn't something to lightly disregard.

George reached for the pants to his tuxedo.

"Wait."

"Who gave it to you?"

"Charles."

Shaking his head, feeling as though he had been hit in the solar plexus, he yanked one leg into his trousers. "Terrific, sweetheart. You'll have to find yourself a local stud. I'm unavailable for part-time service."

"That's a despicable thing to say."

His head jerked up as though she'd clipped him on the jaw. "Saying it doesn't compare with what you're doing. I'm not as sophisticated as you New Yorkers. When I sleep with a woman it's more than just—" He clamped his lips tight to keep from expressing a particularly crude word.

Danielle jerked the coverlet off the bed and wrapped it around her shoulders. She wasn't having any difficulty completing his sentence. The sharp edge of his tongue hurt more than any slip of a knife. She felt as though she were bleeding internally.

"It's a friendship ring. I do not sleep with Charles. I never have."

"Oh yeah? What's wrong? Can't get him to ask you to marry him?"

She couldn't deny the element of truth in

his accusation. She had hinted that she'd be receptive to a marriage proposal from Charles. But back then she hadn't become reacquainted with the man who was trying to break speed records getting dressed.

"So help me, if you tell me dear *old* Charles approves of what has happened between you and me, I'll—" He didn't finish his threat. Her eyes had widened. "I'll be damned," he completed, disgusted with himself.

"Will you cool off and listen?" Danielle blasted. "This morning I talked to Charles."

He left her bed and she had called her boyfriend? Jealousy pounded through him. With one hand George made a slicing motion. "I've heard enough."

Clasping the two sides of the cover together, Danielle stormed toward him, angrily kicking aside the excess material that tangled around her legs. She pitched forward, catching George off balance with what closely resembled a poorly executed body block. Her arms windmilled as she tried to maintain her balance. The last thing she wanted to do was knock him on the bed, then fall all over him.

George grabbed the side of the mattress to keep from pitching both of them on the floor. The top of her head collided with his chin; his teeth sank into his tongue and bottom lip. He clamped his hand over his mouth, moaning with pain and interspersing the moans with curses.

Her pointed chin crashed against his chest.

Air whooshed from her lungs as she slammed against him. Stars swam dizzily in front of her eyes when his chin landed on a haircomb at the crown of her head.

"Oooh!" she yelled, knowing exactly how a shish kebab felt. She pushed off of George's chest, holding her head in her hands. Through blurred vision, she shot him a murderous glance. His face told her that she wasn't the only person knocked silly.

Her clumsiness had caused the accident, but she'd be damned if she'd take the blame. She blamed his hardheadedness for more than the small lump forming on her scalp. Having him flat on his back, speechless, was the best way to maintain his undivided attention.

Leaning across him, her finger peppered his chest to emphasize each word. "Listen to me, you hot-headed, hardheaded Italian. Charles and I are *friends!*"

George tested his tongue by raking it across the roof of his mouth. The tip was completely numb. When he wanted to shout, he was forced to remain silent.

"I promised my *friend* I'd wear the ring." His dark eyes left her face and stared at the ceiling, indicating his disbelief. "It's sort of a talisman. A good-luck ring."

Carefully George touched his bottom lip with his fingers; it wasn't split. Uncertain his tongue wasn't permanently dismembered, he tested it again. The numbness was wearing

135

off. "You love him," he grated, moving his lips and tongue as little as possible.

She wanted to deny loving Charles, but that would be a flagrant lie. She paused as her mind raced.

"Yes, I love Charles." She stopped to keep from saying it wasn't the same way she loved him. He wouldn't believe her. "I love Buffy, too, but I'm not engaged to her!"

"No comparison," he growled, his tongue still smarting. "Buffy is a woman."

"A man and woman can't be friends?" Openhanded, she slammed her hand against the pillow in frustration over his stubborn resistance. "What do you call platonic friends?"

"A polite name for pillow friends."

"That's ridiculous!"

"That's how a man thinks. A man doesn't befriend a beautiful woman without having something else in the back of his mind." George rose, holding Danielle off to one side. He grabbed the phone and put it between them on the bed. "Ask Charles if he's entertained the idea of sharing a pillow with you."

"I can't do that."

"Why not?" Her refusal confirmed his belief. He took her wrist, placing her hand on the phone. "Your friendship with him is supposed to be like your friendship with Buffy. You can ask or tell Buffy anything, can't you?"

"Yes," she admitted. His male logic was defeating her. "Charles and I haven't openly discussed sex. He's too refined."

"Oh, brother," George exclaimed, the flat of his palm striking his forehead. "You traveled the world with him but you've never discussed sharing a bed? That boggles my mind. I can't look at you without thinking about making love."

Danielle twisted the ring on her finger, slowly moving it toward her knuckle. Charles had given her the ring to build her confidence, to shield her from any real or imagined slights, to make her happy. He was a man. Perhaps he'd understand how George perceived the ring. The stone could be fake, but what she felt for George was real. Platonic friendship was beautiful, but love was brilliant in comparison.

The stark paleness of her face twisted his heart. He fought his love, a powerful force that made him want to draw her into his arms and forget about anything other than making love to her. On a physical level they were finely attuned to each other. Professionally they could understand each other and be colleagues. But he couldn't appreciate her concept of friendship. She'd admitted that she loved Charles. In his book, there was only one way a woman loved a man—body and soul. She belonged to him whether she admitted it or not, and he for damned certain wasn't willing to share her with Charles Du Bois.

"I'd better put this in my purse for safekeeping," she said, moving from the bed and picking up her clothes between the bed and the dresser where she'd put her purse. She'd taken off the ring to remove the doubts plagueing George. She had a major doubt of her own that needed clarifying.

She stowed the ring, stalked to the rack where her clothes hung, and put on a blue satin robe. His black eyes followed her until she sat on the edge of the bed. Double-knotting the slippery sash, she asked rhetorically, "Are we friends?"

"Never."

"Enemies?"

"I'm not certain we were ever enemies," he replied, hedging, wondering where she was leading him.

Danielle leaned forward and looked him straight in the eye. "Have you had your revenge or shall we call it quits now?"

CHAPTER EIGHT

"Revenge? Is that what you think I've been up to?" George pulled the sheet to cover himself from the waist down.

"It makes sense. I've given you good reasons for wanting to get back at me."

"Simply demanding an apology would have been easier on me," he grumbled as he stacked the pillows behind his shoulders. Crossing his legs at the ankles he leaned against the cushioned headboard. "I suppose my asking your father for your hand in marriage was the whipped cream and cherry on this diabolical plot of mine?"

His dark eyes penetrated beneath the thick skin she'd tried to grow since she'd used her head as a battering ram. Toughen up, she silently coached. Did she expect him to admit to being a self-made bastard? Anyone capable of emotionally putting her through a meat grinder wasn't going to confess and apologize all in one breath.

"That and announcing our engagement, followed by jilting me at the altar pretty well sprinkles nuts on your concoction," she retorted with her chin inching upward.

"Who put such a crazy idea into your head? Buffy?"

"As I said, it makes sense, doesn't it?"

She ducked her head and raked her hand through her dark curls. Her fingers made a show of blindly searching for the combs that had come loose to avoid implicating her friend. Sometimes George had an uncanny knack of reading her thoughts. She winced as her hand grazed over the small bump on her head. Yesterday he had claimed he wasn't hard-mouthed. The lump on her head proved differently. His chin must be made of steel.

George shook his head. A slow, steady stream of air was exhaled from his lungs. "Why ruin a good theory by stopping there? Why don't I marry you and dedicate my life to making you miserable?"

A pink tinge washed her face. She'd thought of that possibility. It sounded so damned silly when he rephrased her thoughts. "That's carrying revenge too far."

"Oh, I don't know. Any man who'd seduce you for revenge would be capable of wanting to broaden the scope of your misery."

He rubbed his jaw thoughtfully, watching her closely. Her imagination, no doubt with Buffy's vivid contributions, had been running rampant. She'd successfully moved him from the role of arch-rival to the blackest of villains. And yet, less than an hour ago, she'd been a living flame in his hands. She was a hot bundle of contradictions.

"You aren't going to deny the allegations, are you?" Suddenly she felt bone weary. She'd removed Charles's ring, but George refused to remove her doubts. Glancing at him through dark lashes, she saw him touch the tip of his tongue, then grin his off-center smile. "Your tongue is all in one piece. Answer my question."

His smile broadened and his eyes began to sparkle. He winked. "I flatly deny having ulterior motives when I made wild, passionate love with you. I also deny seeking revenge by proposing."

He paused, waiting for that information to sink into her hard head.

Danielle met his eyes. Yes, there was the unmistakable twinkle that seemed to say he was hiding another secret of equal importance. Yes, the black centers were expanding, beckoning her closer. But no, she couldn't see a smidgen of deceit. His cocky, sexy smile made him a lovable scoundrel, but he wasn't lying.

"Then you meant it when—"

"Yes."

"And you aren't—"

"No. When you opened your door and automatically rejected anything I had to offer, I'll admit to wanting to carry you straight to bed. My libido was as hot as a grease fire. I don't know about you, but I've never felt the kind of heat we generate between each other. I have no intention of letting you hop on a plane and fly back to New York without reaching an understanding."

His plain speaking rattled her. She'd prepared herself to listen to a confirmation of her accusation. Thanks to her guilt feelings and Buffy's revenge theory, she'd jumped to the wrong conclusion.

She cleared her throat to make way for the humble pie she'd have to eat. "Well, uh, it looks like I baked a pie without putting the filling inside the crust."

"Looks that way," he agreed, chuckling.

"I'm sorry."

"You should be," George declared, pretending indignation. "You're just lucky you used your verbal spurs on a stallion instead of a horse's ass. But I warn you, stick a bit in my mouth and I'm liable to bite. My tongue is as sore as hell." He held his hand toward her. "I wouldn't object to your kissing it to make it better."

Danielle reluctantly grinned. "Is that your cure for everything? Kissing? Making love?"

"I can't think of a better homemade remedy for a punctured ego—or in this case, a tongue with tooth prints."

She took his hand and willingly moved toward him. He tucked her next to him and brushed the curls from her face.

He heard her contented sigh, then asked, "Who gave you the cock-eyed notion that I had the bit between my teeth and was charging your fences?"

Danielle hated to admit that Buffy instigated the idea. She should have listened to the right side of her brain instead of the left. The guilt, regardless of who voiced the idea first, was hers and hers alone.

"Oh, Dani. It was Buffy, wasn't it?"

She could hear quiet resignation in his question. She felt like a teenager who'd been trading gossip and had been caught whispering lies. She would rather have him scream and shout at her than silently shake his head at her lack of insight as he did.

"One way or another, your friend has always been a problem for us," he said, lightly kissing her brow.

"That's not true. Buffy worshipped the ground you walked on."

"Uh-huh. But that didn't stop her from nipping at my heels." He relaxed, his tension slowly ebbing. "I remember my senior year working up my courage to ask you to the prom. Each time I figured out how to talk to you when you were alone, there she'd be— sweet Buffy. She should have been elected Guard-dog of the Year rather than Sweetest Girl in the class."

"You shocked the letter sweaters off the cheerleaders by taking your next-door neighbor," she supplemented.

"Why would that shock them? Mary

wanted to go. I heard that you were leaving town that weekend, so . . ."

"Mary was . . . fluffy."

"A nice word for plump?"

"Yeah." She snuggled deeper into his arms, loving the way her hip bones pressed against his without any excess poundage between them. "Sounds better than obese, or horror of horrors, F-A-T."

"What would you know about how a *fluffy* person feels?" George scoffed. "You had the sexiest curves of any girl I've met."

"Sexy?" She stared at him as though he'd been standing over the stove too long and was suffering from heat exhaustion.

He slipped his hand into the gaping neckline of her robe and delicately cupped her breast. "Perfect."

Her flesh responded to his light touch immediately. "We're going to be dreadfully late arriving at the restaurant."

"Dreadfully." His lips remained curved as they covered hers. He nibbled her lower lip, saying, "Mario obligingly offered to supervise the kitchen during the dinner hour."

"Then it doesn't make a difference what time we arrive."

"No," he whispered, "that's why I was particular with my clothing. I wanted to rip it off, hop in bed and persuade you . . . ah, Dani." Her tongue swirling around his flat male nipple took the words right out of his mouth. The sheet slowly fell away from him. "Ah, yes, sweetheart."

Her fingers dusted across his stomach, teasing his navel, while she followed the ridges of his rib cage with her lips and tongue. *I love you*, she wrote, spacing each word with a kiss.

By removing her doubts, he'd set her inhibitions free.

Her hand curled around him. She syncopated her strokes with the rise and fall of his chest. Under his expert tutelage she was an apt pupil. Low growls of appreciation mingled with short phrases, telling her how he liked being touched. She could hear his heart pounding wildly, a primitive beat guiding her hand.

She moved over him until he was cradled between her breasts. His stomach shrank beneath her cheek as he filled his starved lungs with air. He arched against her, holding her breasts until they made a natural cradle for him.

She lifted her shoulders and saw his lips stretched tautly across his clenched teeth as he grated, "Danielle . . ."

Her hands settled over his chest, sweetly, hotly.

He knew he should stop her. But nothing in his life had ever felt better. He shuddered heavily.

"I love how you're touching me, sweetheart, but . . ." His hands twined in her curls; his palms framed her face. "It's going to be all over but the shouting unless you stop."

"Shush. Let me pleasure you. Keep telling me what to do, please." Her breath blossomed against his feverish skin. "I love feeling you change, hearing your heart beat faster and faster, knowing you want me more and more. I love the salty taste of your skin." Her tongue sipped along his lowest rib. She nuzzled her face against his stomach. "I love the way you smell. Clean. Spicy. A fragrance that can't be duplicated. I love—"

Danielle caught the word you between her teeth and swallowed it back. Pride kept it from spilling from her mouth.

Incapable of enduring the pleasurable torture, he bodily rolled over until she was pinned beneath him. Feeling her shake beneath him only made him hotter. "Agony and ecstasy," he groaned, moving from one luscious breast to the other. She turned, writhed from side to side, drawing him close. "Weak and strong. Humble and powerful. I've run the gamut of emotions. My head's going to spin off my shoulders."

She tried to speak but couldn't. She was dizzy with love, with wanting.

"I can't wait any longer," he said.

His voice hushed as his teeth worried the tight bud at the tip of her breast. His fingers clamped onto her hips, elevating her to receive his powerful thrust.

With one long stroke he filled her with

splendor. The ragged cry he heard was a sound he'd heard in his dreams of her. He held her motionless; her body changing, adapting to him. With the thick taste of joy on his tongue, he moved, slowly, giving her full range of the intimate sensations, and then gradually increasing the tempo as his thumb teased the flowering bud within her softness until she shivered with ecstasy.

Danielle's body was no longer hers; it truly belonged to George. He'd taken it—one glance, one whisper, one caress, one kiss at a time. His mouth swallowed her low whimpers, devouring them, consuming her inner fire. The world shattered around her, showering scintillating sparks of flame over them.

She didn't hear him claim her as his own. Nor was she able to read his lips as he throbbed, pulsated, then burst. "I love you, Dani. I swear by all that's holy, I love you."

Danielle opened her eyes, feeling as though she'd been torn apart and put back together with serenity as the adhesive. She stretched in contentment. Sometime during the void between the earth shattering and her return to full awareness George had covered her with the bedspread.

Shifting her head, she saw his head sharing the same pillow. His fabulous black eyes were closed. He breathed peacefully.

"Asleep?" she whispered.

"No. I think I've died and gone to heaven."

"That good?" she fished.

"That awesome," he corrected. He yawned, politely covering his mouth with his hand. "When are you moving back to Williamsburg?"

Grinning, Danielle teased, "Oh, I've heard 1990 is supposed to be a good year."

"No problem. What's your address in New York?"

"Why?"

"Because you're either moving here or I need to know where to have the postmaster send my mail. We aren't going to be apart three days, much less three years."

She propped her head in her hand and traced his lips with one fingernail. "Do you plan on asking my Dad if it's okay for you to move in with me?"

"I'd prefer to make things legal, but I'm adaptable. Get this in your head, sweetheart. I'm sticking to you like wet spaghetti in a dry pan. You can scrape and scratch, but I'll be there clinging to you."

"Hmm." Collapsing on his chest, she whispered, "Limp noodle—that's exactly how I feel. Boneless. Something you could wrap around your finger for safekeeping."

"So? Do you want me to go to New York with you to help pack?" he persisted.

"I'll have to think about it."

"Five seconds long enough?" His hand curved low on her hips. "One Mississippi, two Mississippi—"

"Do you want me to stay here and help you pack?" she asked as she ended his counting by sealing his lips with her finger.

"Sure. Packing up my stuff won't take long. Ten, maybe fifteen years or so. Locating a vacant lot in the heart of Manhattan should be a snap. About as easy as moving a two-story brick building from Virginia to New York. No problem."

"George!"

"Danielle!" he mimicked. "It's taken years to build Garavelli's reputation and clientele. Your business is portable."

"You make mine sound like a hot-dog stand that I roll down Fifth Avenue at the end of the day."

George chuckled at her understatement, then countered, "It's not as though you were moving to a strange city where you didn't know anyone. This is your hometown."

"My parents are moving."

"Buffy is here," he said and then groaned, uncertain of whether that was good or bad news.

"If it weren't impossible, I'd swear you were jealous of my best friend."

He realized Danielle was closer to the truth than she realized. Jealousy was a close relative of envy. God knew he had envied Buffy. Being privy to Danielle's childhood thoughts and teenage dreams was an enviable position he'd been denied.

"Are my eyes green?" He opened one eye

149

and held up his hand. "Feel me. Not one jealous bone."

"Humph!" A wicked light twinkled in her eyes. She no longer believed the revenge theory, but she damned well knew his reaction to Charles's ring was too adamant to be anything but jealousy. She'd eaten humble pie without choking. What George Garavelli needed was a double serving. "What about Charles?"

George's self-esteem slipped a notch, but he hung on to it by answering, "Purely a moral principle. What would you think if you'd heard I was sniffing around some little filly that had another man's brand on her rump?" His hand playfully scampered over her flank as though he were checking for a fleur-de-lis.

"Then you wouldn't object to me going into business with him, would you?" she crooned, wriggling as he tickled her.

He had other plans, but he wanted Danielle to see for herself how well they could work together, how happy they'd be sharing a common goal, which would be to make Garavelli's the finest Italian restaurant on the East Coast.

"Starting a new business is risky," he dissuaded, hoping she'd offer to assist him.

"Put Du Bois in neon lights and watch the people flock to stand in line to wait for a table. Besides, Charles is putting up the money. All I'm risking is my time."

George had strong convictions about having another man spend money on his future wife. He swallowed his pride and protests, then smiled. "Old Charles may retract his offer once he realizes you aren't going to be Countess Dani, or whatever the hell your title would be."

Danielle tossed her head back and crowed, "You are jealous! You just proved it!"

"Okay. Maybe a little jealous," he replied grudgingly.

"How much?" she teased, rewarding him for his admission by peppering kisses on his cheeks.

"Bushels. Tons," he amended. "Happy?"

"Deliriously." She hugged him with all her might. "Beyond measure."

He kissed her and tasted her happiness. It was a delectable blending of his flavor and hers that was more heady than champagne, sweeter than honey, wilder than the desire he'd contained for years. "Ready to face the Garavelli family?"

Gracefully, Danielle tossed the covers aside and rose. "That depends. Are the Garavellis going to put me on the grill. Buffy was."

"Maybe." Odds were that he'd be the one roasted. "I have an emergency escape planned."

She glanced over her shoulder as she picked up her dress. George was still in bed, watching her as though she were a luscious banquet table being prepared for a connoisseur. Her skin tingled as she felt his eyes ingest her. She snapped her fingers to get his attention.

"Oh, yeah, I'm supposed to get dressed too." He gradually moved from the bed into the bathroom, lingering long enough to take one last look.

"What emergency plan?" she cued, laughing at his reluctance, but silently glorying in knowing he wanted to stay exactly where he'd been.

George sniffed. Her fragrance clung to his skin. Not only did they taste alike, they smelled the same. He hesitated, then turned on the faucet and rinsed. His family would razz him unbearably if he came in smelling of her perfume.

"You could faint," he suggested, raising his voice to be heard over the splashing water in the sink. "I'll do the manly thing. Swoop you into my arms and carry you to the nearest bed."

"Uh-huh. The second part sounds inviting, but what happens if somebody sticks spirits of ammonia under my nose? We both know a chef would be out of business if their olfactory glands were destroyed."

Laughing, he hitched a towel low on his hips and strode back into the bedroom. "I did consider having you dump a plate of food on my lap, but the dry cleaners can't remove the stain tomato paste leaves." Lovely, he thought, watching her smile as her eyes followed him in the mirror. "I also considered hitting the fire alarm, but the last time one of the employees did that the fire department hacked a hole in the roof over the charcoal grill. Ever try to light a gas grill when it's submerged in water?"

"No, but I did have a smoke alarm start buzzing once. Flambe. I poured the brandy over the cherries, struck a match, and poof!" Her eyes clung to the spot in the mirror that reflected where he'd casually tucked the towel in. She blinked to still her active imagination. One little tug, both sides of her brain sang in harmony. Just one.

"What happened?"

Her eyes raised and caught the amusement flickering in his. Flustered, she stammered, "Sirens wailing, the fire department arrived ready to extinguish dinner. Charles spent ten minutes convincing them I wasn't a pyromaniac intent on burning down the mansion. That evening my face was considerably hotter than the food I served."

"You're lucky someone didn't dump a box of salt in it," he quipped, making a funny face as he imagined the flavor of salted cherries. His eyes remained on her reflection as he pulled on his pants, zippered and snapped them. He had his shirt on before he saw the smirk on Danielle's face. He unsnapped, unzipped, and tucked his shirttail in the waistband. "You're distracting," he said, grinning foolishly at his mistake. He stepped closer.

"You'd have less trouble with that lacy piece of nothing if you didn't have it on inside out."

Danielle glanced down at her fumbling fingers and heard him hoot with laughter. She was putting it on correctly, but it was pure luck. Good-naturedly she accepted his lively sense of humor and said, "We'd better check each other's clothing carefully before we leave. I'd hate to arrive with a designer's label under my chin and you with your fly open."

"My brothers would love speculating about where I've been and what we've been doing."

She blushed at the thought of his family knowing. Unsophisticated attitude, she decided, sauntering into the bathroom to freshen up her makeup. On close inspection, she realized that wearing her clothes with the label displayed like a placard wouldn't be any more revealing than the starry-eyed look in her eyes. Passion had left a pouty imprint on her mouth that only time would erase. The sandpaper texture of his skin had buffed her skin until it glowed. Yes, she looked like a woman who'd been thoroughly loved and there wasn't a damned thing she could do to hide it.

Women in love were supposed to be radiant, she thought by way of explanation.

"I'm missing a stud," George said from the adjoining room. Thinking a particularly lusty thought, she laughed as she heard him call, "Never mind. I've got it."

"Yes, my love, you'll get no argument from

154

me." She giggled into her washcloth, remembering the popular slang term for a good-looking guy during her high school years. She'd lost her cookie ration for a week when she'd said it in front of her mother.

He was dressed and waiting when she walked from the bathroom. Other than his bow tie matching the tilt of his smile, he looked suave and debonair. She straightened his tie; her hands lingered on his shoulders as she gave a heartfelt sigh.

"What's wrong?"

She lifted one shoulder, unable to explain the qualms she felt. She pivoted on one foot and moved to the dresser. Careful not to muss her hair, she pulled the white dress over her head.

George picked up the pearls and latched the clasp at her nape. "Don't worry about meeting my family. You aren't a stranger they haven't heard about."

That's exactly what worried her. She knew what they'd heard from his very lips. In his brothers' minds she was Bubble-butt, the kid who caused their sibling one headache after another.

CHAPTER NINE

Preconceived notions were invariably wrong, Danielle thought as George led her into Garavelli's kitchen through the back door. The aroma of onions, garlic, oregano, and basil permeated the air, making her mouth water. A two-foot-long pan of lasagna being removed from the oven was almost enough food to quiet her nervous stomach.

Unobserved by the chefs and helpers, her wide eyes scanned the room. She didn't have any concrete reason for believing the kitchen would be outdated, but she was genuinely surprised at the gleaming white-tiled walls, the stainless steel pots and pans hanging from a revolving rack over a wooden butcher's block, and the latest in computerized scales to accurately measure ingredients. Small television cameras were strategically mounted to keep an eye on the kitchen operation from the business office.

The Garavellis didn't have to worry about the health department putting a B sticker on their front window. Everything was immaculate from the meat grinder to the walk-in refrigerator.

George beamed when he heard her mumble, "I'm impressed. I had no idea that your kitchen would be this modern, and organized."

"I know what you expected." His low chuckle brought a pink tinge to her cheeks. "Frankly, if you'd visited the place three years ago, your suspicions would have been verified. We expanded by purchasing the building next door. I've poured every available penny back in to the business. Come and see the office, then I'll take you into the dining room and introduce you to everyone."

She followed him as he skirted the back wall and climbed the steps leading to the second floor.

His hand swept in a wide arc around a storage area neatly stacked with paper and canned goods. "Should the need for additional space arise, I've had an architect draw plans that would open the front part of the room as a balcony overlooking the main dining room."

"Business must be flourishing under your guidance," she murmured, eyeing the century-old brick, mentally picturing the conversion and the problems it would create.

Transporting food from the kitchen could easily be solved with a dumbwaiter. A short partition wall along the back of the room would block off the customers' view of trays, dishes, and silverware. Overhead lighting should be dim, she mused. Dropping the ceiling and installing an electrical version of flickering candles would lend a sense of coziness. Partitions in unlikely places would provide small nooks and crannies for privacy.

Danielle curbed the temptation to fine-tune the mental image she'd created by decorating the imaginary tables with bud vases, linens, and crystal stemware. This wasn't her restaurant. When Charles had discussed a business venture, they had planned on building something sleek, something unique that would set their establishment apart from the historical flavor of other food businesses in the area.

"During the tourist season we could use the extra seating capacity," George continued. "But from October through April I'd have to rely on private parties and community functions to make it pay." He frowned, stopping in front of a partially open oak door. "Wonder who's in here," he thought aloud as he pushed it open.

He stepped aside, gesturing for her to precede him into the office.

"I'd thought you'd be making the table rounds downstairs," he said to his mother, who was seated in a swivel chair directly in front of four television screens. "Mother, this is Danielle Brewster."

Isobelle Garavelli destroyed another preconceived notion. For some unfathomable

158

reason she had pictured George's mother as short and rotund, with laugh wrinkles etching the corners of her eyes. The stereotype of Moma Garavelli shattered. The tall, slender woman, elegantly garbed in a fashionable black dress with her white hair swept away from her classic features took Danielle by surprise. She hadn't expected to be warmly embraced as though she were an old family friend, but the cool speculation in Isobelle's brown eyes raised the short hairs on Danielle's nape. Only when Isobelle's face turned toward her son did Danielle see a softening of her aristocratic features.

George dutifully crossed the room and kissed her on both cheeks. Other men might have been embarrassed to kiss their mother, but he wasn't. Obviously, Isobelle had trained her sons well.

He whispered in his mother's ear, bringing a smile to her lips and an affectionate pat to his cheek. Love and mutual respect flowed easily between mother and son.

"Welcome to Garavelli's," Isobelle formally greeted Danielle, extending her hand toward a creamy leather sofa and matching chair. "Giorgio, why don't you check on the problem at station five, then bring Ms. Brewster and me a glass of white wine?"

Danielle had heard a similar ring of command in the voice of an Arab sheikh who'd been born to rule over the masses. A wry smile twisted her lips as she seated herself at the far corner of the sofa. Much to her amusement, she watched George obediently follow his mother's orders, pausing only long enough to wink at her before he closed the door.

"Giorgio tells me the two of you have common interests," Isobelle said, gracefully crossing the thick carpet and sitting on the edge of the chair directly opposite Danielle.

"The restaurant business?" Danielle asked, her voice high due to nervous tension. A curt nod from Isobelle indicated she expected Danielle to elaborate. "I've studied with Charles Du Bois for the last seven years."

"Ah," Isobelle replied, easing back into the expensive leather. A small but genuine smile curved her lips. "I've heard Giorgio speak of him. The French version of the Galloping Gourmet?"

At least she has a sense of humor, Danielle thought, returning the smile. " 'Have pots, will travel' is Charles's favorite motto."

She heard Isobelle's soft laughter and wondered how detailed a report George had filed with his mother. Everything from the hateful nickname to his unexpected dinner date the other night, she surmised. Her little finger nudged her ring finger as she wished her lucky talisman were in place. Had it been on her finger rather than in her purse, she knew she'd be making several heartfelt wishes.

"Will Mr. Du Bois be returning to Williamsburg with you?" Isobelle inquired.

Her near-white eyebrow arched, but Danielle noticed a slight tremor pass through the hand she had casually draped on the chair's arm. Isobelle was as uncomfortable as she was herself, Danielle realized, amazed by the discovery. What had George told her? He'd made pointed remarks concerning her snobbishness on three occasions. Were they both trying to impress each other by appearing sophisticated while quivering like mousse on the inside? This supremely standoffish woman couldn't have mothered four sons, run a restaurant while raising them, and have a reputation for wanting grandchildren if her heart was a solid block of ice.

"You'd love Charles," she said, deciding to chip a corner off the iceberg. Mentally she matched the widow Garavelli with Charles and found herself liking the picture. "Ellie, my mother, didn't wash the hand Charles kissed for weeks."

Isobelle's mouth twitched as though she wanted to make a spicy retort. Her lips thinned as she maintained control. "I'm certain Mr. Du Bois is charming if he's a friend of yours," she replied politely.

"And witty," Danielle added, watching Isobelle's face for her reaction. "Handsome, too. About your age, I imagine. How old are you, Isobelle?"

Her audacity broke through the ice. Isobelle leaned forward and patted her hand in the same manner she'd patted her son's cheek. "My dear Danielle, any woman who tells her age has no other secrets worth divulging."

Danielle's eyes merrily twinkled in response to the mild rebuke. She lightly squeezed the older woman's hand and said, "Well, I guess I'm in big trouble. Your son knows exactly how old I am."

"Yes, but you've always been a mystery to him," she contradicted, her smile warm and inviting. "I remember him rushing through the kitchen, demanding that his father and I attend a dancing recital my niece was participating in, and take him along. Throughout the performance, I watched him. His eyes were fascinated by a girl with long, dark banana curls tied in a pink satin ribbon. Do you know what he announced to his father as we walked to the ice cream parlor?"

"That he wanted to join ballet classes?" Danielle teased, uncertain she wanted to hear what he had said.

Isobelle laughed at the idea of her thin, lanky child swaggering around in tights. "No. He said he'd seen the girl he was going to marry." She laughed at Danielle's comical twist of her mouth. "Then he promptly asked if his father would give him two dollars to buy an ice cream sundae for him and his girlfriend."

Groaning, Danielle recalled how George had left the ice cream parlor wearing more than he'd eaten. Isobelle's melodic laughter reminded Danielle of wind chimes, pleasing to her ear.

Hearing footsteps on the stair treads, Isobelle whispered, "You'll understand if I don't recommend the homemade spumoni, won't you?"

George balanced a tray holding three goblets of wine on a serving tray and listened at the door. Dead silence. He'd left knowing both women were uncommonly stiff and ill at ease, but surely they hadn't stared daggers at each other the entire time he'd been gone.

He glanced at the tray, suddenly wishing he'd brought the entire bottle.

"I'm back," he announced with a flourish of the linen napkin he'd placed on his arm. He couldn't read a damned thing on either his mother's or Danielle's face. He served his mother first, but gave Danielle a quizzical look. She responded to his expression with a benign smile that could mean anything from your-mother-is-a-witch to what-a-lovely-woman. He placed her drink on a small cocktail napkin and tried to see beneath the fringe of lashes she'd lowered over her eyes. "So, how are my two favorite women getting along?" he asked with a cheerfulness he wasn't feeling.

While George had his back to his mother, Isobelle made a shivering gesture, then winked.

"Fine," they chorused in unison.

"Did Mother tell you about the plans for

your parents' farewell party?" he asked, wondering what the hell had taken place while he'd been gone.

"No, she didn't," Danielle replied, refusing to add to his chit-chat.

"Did you tell her about traveling from place to place, cooking for the rich and famous?"

"No," Isobelle replied, rescuing Danielle from his piercing black eyes. Certain her arrogant son assumed she'd been extolling his virtues, she added, "She did mention Charles Du Bois though."

You discussed Charles—with my mother? his eyes flashed in Danielle's direction. He raised his wineglass and took a large gulp.

Danielle sipped her wine to keep from giggling. Isobelle Garavelli was as irascible as her nephew Mario. There was no doubt in her mind that his mother kept George on his toes while she cracked the whip. Considering George's good looks and charm, that was probably what had kept him from being a conceited playboy.

She didn't mind conspiring with Isobelle to tweak her son's nose, but she didn't want to put it out of joint. George had admitted to being jealous of Charles.

"We were about to go to the dining room," Danielle said, rising and watching as George offered his mother a helping hand.

"I'm sorry I can't join you for dinner," Isobelle addressed Danielle, glancing at her watch. "I have guests from Charleston visiting that I promised to dine with this evening. I'd recommend something from the open flame broiler." She cast a meaningful look at her son's backside. "Rump roast?"

Danielle chuckled, knowing perfectly well that a rump roast was too tough to flame broil.

"Tony, Alberto, and Dennis, my other sons, are looking forward to meeting you," Isobelle added.

"Don't forget Mario and Buffy," George said, completing the list with a slight grimace.

"It should be an interesting evening," his mother concluded, her voice barely concealing a bubble of laughter. "Very interesting."

Interesting was a classic bit of understatement, Danielle thought, grinning as George squirmed in the chair beside her. Within seconds of arriving in the dining room, the Garavelli brothers, with Mario and Buffy, had descended on them.

Her head reeled from the extravagant compliments Tony and Alberto paid her. Dennis, barely eighteen, watched her with his shy, soulful eyes as though each word she uttered contained great pearls of wisdom.

Tony, Bert, and Mario compensated for their youngest brother's silence by telling stories about Giorgio, pounding nails in his coffin with glee. The more George squirmed and protested, the louder they heckled him. She fully expected one of the Garavelli rogues to

165

present her with a photograph of a bare baby on a bear rug.

George ground his back molars, attempting to smile, but falling short of anything beyond a tight-lipped grimace. Within five minutes, the pack of them had gone beyond exaggeration and made a beeline toward bawdy fiction. He deserved being roasted by his siblings. He couldn't deny telling his share of windy stories in reversed situations, but nonetheless, he'd mentally rescheduled the duty roster for the next ten years.

His older brother, Tony, would be placed in charge of making spinach noodles until his face turned green. Bert would love operating the dishwashing machine for the next decade. And Mario? He didn't have to worry about producing the first Garavelli baby; he'd be on night duty for the next century!

Buffy excused both herself and Danielle for a trip to the powder room.

"Whew!" Buffy fanned her face with both hands. "The brothers are frying George, aren't they? I'm glad the heat is off Mario for a change. How did you get along with Isobelle?"

Danielle removed her lipstick from her purse, answering, "Fine, I suppose. Ten minutes with her and I know where the men got their devilish sense of humor."

"Hey, kiddo, I wasn't laughing when she asked me if I'd ordered birth announcements at the same time I ordered wedding invitations." Buffy ran a comb through her tawny hair. "Point blank she asked me if twins ran in my family. Twins, for Pete's sake! Mario is her nephew. Just think, she'll probably expect triplets from you."

"We didn't discuss babies," Danielle said, tracing the natural curve of her lip with lipstick.

"She's probably on my case because Mario told her he'd probably accept the chef position at the Trellis."

"He what? George will be furious. Why is Mario leaving the family business?"

Buffy shrugged. "Job security. He's no fool, Danielle. It's pretty obvious that when you marry Giorgio, Mario would be scouring the want ads. There's an opening now, but later there may not be."

"He's jumping to conclusions then. Has either of you given thought to the possibility of George moving to New York?"

Buffy stared at Danielle. "Did he say he would?"

"No. But the days of women throwing their careers aside to meekly follow the paths their husbands forge is from a bygone era." Danielle snapped the cover on the tube. "Who knows? I might take Charles up on his offer to open a high-class French restaurant here in Williamsburg."

Groaning, Buffy shook her head. "Listen to me, Danielle Brewster, I'll admit, I *may* have jumped to the wrong conclusion regarding why Giorgio was interested in you, but Isobelle isn't going to tolerate having her son ride off into the sunset on the back of your horse. That simply isn't done in Italian westerns."

"George isn't an only child," Danielle argued. "There are three other sons . . . and Mario to consider."

"Tony may be the oldest, but Giorgio is the driving force of this operation. He's the one that keeps the other brothers in line."

"I didn't notice any of them toeing the line a few minutes ago. George looked hot enough to stick dry spaghetti under their fingernails."

"That's expected. Mario was practically spitting cooking utensils the first night we came here. You've missed the key to the Garavelli logic," Buffy said, pointing her comb and shaking it at Danielle. "It's perfectly okay for them to batter the walls down with each other's heads from the inside, but woe unto any outsider who dares to even rattle a windowpane."

Danielle plucked the comb from Buffy's fingers. "Come on, Buffy. That's as archaic as the revenge theory."

"Oh, yeah? Well, test this theory out, why don't you? Go back out there and tell everyone George will be joining you in New York. Talk about rattling windowpanes. They'll treat you like a wrecking crew that's arrived with a demolition ball."

"It's not my place to tell the Garavellis what

future plans George and I are making. They're his family."

"Humph! A little birdie told me that George announced your betrothal to your parents *before* you did. What's the difference between you telling his family and him telling yours?"

"None. But . . ."

Buffy laughed, rolling her eyes toward the ceiling. "I'm the one who has an IQ that would fill a gallon jar and barely enough common sense to fill a shot glass. You're the one who's supposed to be intelligent and have a level head on your shoulders."

"Why spoil the sauce by adding lumps? I know you're wrong this time," she said, displaying more confidence than she felt.

Danielle twisted several ringlets around her finger, smoothing the comb around the edges. Buffy was wrong. After all, she and George had discussed who was going to live where. He'd voiced some opposition, saying her business was portable and his wasn't, but that wasn't a flat refusal. He'd told her he was adaptable. Maybe not in the same context, but a man was either rigid or flexible regardless of the topic under consideration. He'd also told her they weren't going to be apart three days, much less three years when she'd teased him. She'd found three specific instances that were solid proof for what she believed.

"What makes you so certain? Has he told

you something the rest of the family doesn't know yet?" Buffy moved closer, taking her by the arm. "This affects my life, too. Mario may take the other job, but deep down I know he'd rather stay with the family."

Confiding in her long-time friend was second nature to Danielle, so she didn't hesitate to say, "George said he wasn't going to let me out of his sight. That if I went to New York, he'd be right behind me."

"Do you honestly think he'd stay there with you?" Buffy covered her mouth with her hand. Her eyes widened, horrified by what she'd been thinking. "What am I doing? I'm pushing you out of Williamsburg, aren't I? You must think I'm awful!" she wailed.

"Buffy, I don't think you're awful." She gave her a quick hug. "You're going to marry Mario. There'd be something wrong with you if you valued our friendship more than your love for Mario."

She'd learned that lesson the hard way when she'd removed Charles's ring.

"Damn," Buffy grumbled, blinking her eyes rapidly. "My contact slipped. I swear, the first thing I'm going to do after the honeymoon is throw them in the trash can."

Shaking her head, Danielle chuckled. "And what's Mario going to say?"

"He told me he thinks I'm cute with my glasses on," she sniffed. She reached into her purse to get a tissue. "I love him, Dani. He makes me feel—"

"Wonderful. I know that feeling." She hugged Buffy. "It's okay. Dry your eyes."

"Do you think, if the opportunity arose, that I might mention the possibility of George moving to New York?"

Danielle would have felt rotten if she refused. "No. But try to be tactful. Okay?"

"I swear, Dani, you're the best friend I've ever had."

For some strange reason, Danielle knew she was going to eat her friend's words long before she walked down the aisle at Buffy's wedding. What she didn't realize was that George would be stuffing them down her mouth within the next half hour.

"Did you have to tell Buffy we discussed where we'd be living?" George demanded, thoroughly out of sorts with his family and Danielle Brewster. All hell had broken loose when Buffy hinted that Mario could take the chef's position at Garavelli's because there was a good chance Danielle and he wouldn't be staying in Williamsburg.

She scooted to the far side of the bench seat and hugged the passenger door. "Buffy is my friend. You're acting as if I'd given a secret recipe to your competitors."

"I warned you about your nasty habit of selective listening. You hear what you want to hear and discard the rest as unimportant."

"Such as?"

"I told you it would take ten or twenty years for me to pack up my belongings and

171

move to New York. I explicitly told you that your job was portable and mine required starting from scratch."

"Are you telling me you won't consider moving to New York?" she snapped.

"I'm telling you I can't pack up and travel around the world like your friend Charles. I have family obligations. Responsibilities."

Her eyes narrowed to small slits as she took in what he was saying. "I don't want to victimize you with my nasty habit, so would you answer my questions with a simple yes or no?" she asked with a deathly calm tone. He hesitated, then nodded. Her mind raced to make a priority list. "Do you love me?"

"Of course I love you," he bellowed. "Would I ask a woman to be my wife, bear my children if I didn't love her?"

"A simple yes or no."

"Yes," he hissed, starting the car and peeling from the parking lot. That wasn't how he'd planned on telling her. He had wanted to wait for the right moment. Either he'd missed his chance when he'd been too tongue-tied with passion, or the right time hadn't occurred. Disgusted with himself, he added in a calmer voice, "I love you, Dani. I always have."

She heard his tone soften, saw the regret in his eyes, but she forced herself to continue. "Are you forbidding me to exchange confidences with my trusted friends?"

"Of course not. I just don't want something

we've discussed privately blabbed around town before we've made a final decision. How do you think my mother is going to feel when she hears Tony or Bert talk about me leaving?"

Danielle cupped her hand to her ear. "Sorry. I didn't hear your reply. Was that a yes or a no?"

"Ah, sweetheart. That's like asking me if I quit beating my dog. If I say yes, then I've admitted to animal cruelty. If I say no, then you can assume I'm still beating the dog. Either way, I lose. Would you rephrase the question?"

"No."

"You're being unreasonable."

"Yes." He might not be able to answer with a simple yes or no, but she could. "Are you forbidding me to exchange confidences with my trusted friends?"

George wrenched the wheel, cutting a corner too quickly. The tires squealed in protest. He fought to keep control of the car and his tongue, which was still tender to the touch. By God, if she can be hardheaded, so could he, he decided. "Yes!"

"Terrific," she muttered, turning her face toward the side window and wondering how she'd look with her mouth stitched closed. She knew the answer to her last question before it tumbled from her mouth. "Will you move to New York City and live with me?"

"Danielle, please sweetheart, be reasonable. I can't walk away from a business I've poured my heart and soul into because of a crazy whim. You talked about moving back to Williamsburg, remember? Now you're being stubborn."

"Yes. Should I repeat that question also?"

"No."

"No, you don't want the question repeated or—"

"No. I can't permanently move to New York." His shoulders sagged. "I can't."

He thought about demanding three questions of his own, but he knew it would be a waste of energy. The situation was out of his control.

She loved him. She would confide in Buffy or Charles, or whomever else she'd befriended. And he'd lay money, he couldn't pry her out of New York with a crowbar.

Impasse. He couldn't give; she wouldn't give.

The remainder of the drive was completed in a silence that had a deafening quality. Perhaps the sound of their love exploding into thin air had destroyed his hearing. He didn't know and was past caring. He was losing Danielle. That was all he could comprehend.

Danielle surreptitiously wiped away the tear tracking down her cheek. She wouldn't cry. Not now, Not here. George Garavelli swore he wasn't seeking revenge, but he'd gotten it. He'd been a heartbreaker all his life.

Why had she been so foolish as to believe he wouldn't break hers?

She unsnapped her purse. The wish ring, her good-luck talisman, sparkled as the stone gathered a minuscule amount of light. Without hesitating, she put it back on her finger. She needed every ounce of luck it contained to get her through the next twenty-four hours, to get her out of Williamsburg and back to New York where she'd be safe.

George racked his brain for a solution. He parked his car and turned off the engine. "One of us is making a terrible mistake," he said, wearily smoothing his brow.

"Yes."

"Knock it off, will you?"

"Why? Yes and no answers should suit you. Everything is black and white. There's nothing in between. A woman can have friends, but only if they're other women. A man can be a lover, but never, never a friend. A woman should keep her mouth shut and follow in the oversized footprints of her man." Danielle took a deep breath, then sighed. "I'm the wrong woman for you, George. You're the wrong man for me."

"Dammit, I know we're right for each other. Is it going to take another twenty-eight years for you to realize it? You don't want a wimp any more than I want a submissive wife. We both have tempers. We're going to fight tooth and nail. We aren't mismatched!"

She gave him a mockery of a smile. "We're

175

too much alike. That's why we competed with each other in high school. That's why we're both in the same business. We make beautiful sparks when we strike against each other, but we can't get along for a weekend. We would be making a terrible mistake unless we can salvage something. If we could part as—oh hell, we can't even be friends." She unlatched her door and stepped from the car. "Good night."

"Good night? That sounded like good-bye," he muttered, opening his door and running after her. "Danielle, wait!"

There was no waiting.

"I'm not going to grovel," he bellowed. "A Garavelli doesn't beg! If you walk through that door, I won't—" His threat died an ignoble death on his lips. Hands on his hips, he cursed himself for being seven kinds of a fool.

CHAPTER TEN

Within an hour, George was close to being blitzed. He rarely drank, never alone, and he seldom ordered straight Scotch on the rocks. His brothers warily circled him, but none of them were willing to risk having their noses broken. One more and he would crawl up the back steps and pass out on the sofa in the office, he decided fuzzily. He signaled Joe, the bartender, by raising his empty glass.

"Stupid fight," he muttered against the rim of his glass. "Should've kept my mouth shut."

"Uh, boss," Joe stammered. He towered over George and was twice as brawny, but Joe had been in the business long enough to know when not to push a man. George Garavelli had the look of a man who had pushed himself to the limits. "Don't you think . . ."

"Don't wanna think. Pour me another, then leave me alone. Got it?" The fire burning deep in his eyes was meant to be heeded. No, he didn't want to think or feel. As soon as the world stopped spinning, he'd get off. "Blew it. One chance and I blew it."

"Rough night?" a stranger asked sympathetically.

"Yeah." He tried to focus his eyes on the man's face. Six eyes, three noses, and a multitude of lips. All of them rotating in different directions. Must not be a regular customer, George thought, mildly amused. "Ever been in love?"

"Passionately. Once. A long time ago," the kindly gentleman replied. "When you get to be my age friendship is more important than passion."

George leaned forward. Being closer didn't help his eyes focus. The stranger didn't look old. He'd talked kind of funny, but if he got rid of the extra eyeballs, he'd be almost normal. "You're not old, are ya?"

"Sixty, give or take a few months. What's her name?"

"Danielle." Her name rolled off his lips wistfully. "Brewster. I'm crazy in love with her." He laughed at himself. "Right now, I think I'm just plain old crazy. Can I buy you a drink?"

"No, thank you. Pardon me for saying so, but I don't think you need another one, either."

"You're pardoned." An untimely hiccup and a sheepish grin later, he added, "Pardon me, too."

"Why don't you go home and get some sleep? You'll feel better tomorrow."

"I'm gonna sleep here. My family owns

Garavelli's. Best Italian restaurant in Williamsburg." His hand waggled toward the entrance. "See Mario over there? He's a lousy relative but he makes great pizza. My crummy brothers are around here somewhere too. We all work here. Wanted her here, too."

"Is the attractive silver-haired woman standing near the grand piano related to you?"

George straightened without turning around on the bar stool to look at her. The family had a strict policy regarding being inebriated on the premises: Don't. "Isobelle. My mother."

"She looks worried."

"Believe it or not, I don't usually drink. She's waiting for me to fall off the stool, then she's going to kick me for making a horse's ass out of myself."

The older man grinned. "Madame doesn't look like the kicking type."

"Madame?" George repeated, slurring the accent. "Mademoiselle? She's a widow. Is a widow a madame or a mademoiselle?" Pleased that he'd put together a three-syllable word, he chuckled, missing his new-found friend's reply. "I wanted Dani and I . . . me? . . . the two of us, to be like Mom and Dad used to be. Working together. Laughing. Loving. Wanted to share everything. God, I love her."

"Does she love you?"

George pondered the question. She did. She had to love him. "Yes."

"Then what's the problem?"

"I'm black and white—she's everything in between. Jeez, that doesn't make sense. Makes me sound like a tablecloth, huh?" His friend laughed. George recognized the sound. It belonged to some famous movie star. "You a famous actor?"

"No."

"Hmm. Would I recognize you if I were sober?"

"Maybe." The stranger motioned with his gold-tipped cane for two of the Garavelli brothers to assist him. "You've a big party booked for tomorrow. I've arranged for someone to help you upstairs."

"Dan and Ellie," George mumbled, beyond resisting his brothers' assistance. "You know 'em?"

The stranger grinned. "I'm an old friend of the Brewster family. And now, my young friend, let me give you a friendly piece of unsolicited advice. Don't let foolish pride stand between you and your destiny."

George grinned, falling limply into his brothers' arms. "My pride already goeth. It's my self-respect that's in the dest—dust."

Charles watched the Garavelli brothers none too gently help their brother. He reached for his billfold. A well-manicured hand stopped him from placing the green bills on the bar.

"Be my guest," Isobelle offered. "I appreciate you talking some sense into my son. I'm afraid I wasn't available when his brothers got their mouths rolling earlier this evening. I'm Isobelle Garavelli."

"Charles Du Bois." His beguiling eyes met hers levelly as he raised her hand to his lips. An almost, but not quite forgotten pulse of electricity tingled from his lips to the region surrounding his heart. "Would you join me for a nightcap?"

Dressed in her spangled, feathered designer's creation, Danielle inspected the illusion the dress created. Satisfied she couldn't do anything further to hide her puffy eyes, she braced her shoulder, lifted her chin, and headed to the door. Her parents' farewell party would be a gruesome ordeal, but she'd done her best to disguise her inner turmoil.

The one bright spot in her day had been Charles's surprise arrival. He would be her escort. She needed all the moral support she could get. When Charles had called earlier, she'd felt as though a ray of sunshine had peeked through storm clouds.

Whether George Garavelli liked it or not, Charles was her friend. Maybe, with Charles and Buffy standing on each side of her, she wouldn't resort to misbehaving to get George's attention.

Oh yes, she'd done some long hard thinking during the night. From the ice cream stunt right on through to ramming her head into his chin, she'd been doing everything to make George notice her.

When she'd finally accomplished her objective, she had been too scared of failing in the future to accept success. Subconsciously she had thrown stumbling blocks between them to ensure her failure. Finally, she'd pushed George into a corner, where he had to come out swinging or lose everything he'd gained professionally.

She waved at Charles as she saw him enter the lobby. A flash later, she was being kissed on both cheeks and hugged.

"You look fabulous, *ma petite*," Charles complimented her, his eyes roaming from her silver heels to her silver eyeshadow. Aware that she'd had a sleepless night, he added, "Your eyes look as though the sandman slept in them."

"Yours look like you swallowed the sun. If I didn't know better, I'd think you were in love."

He shrugged, twirled his cane, and kept silent. He'd promised himself not to play Cupid or arm Danielle with bow and arrows.

"You're going to pop if you don't tell me your secret. Charles Du Bois, what have you been up to while I've been away?"

"Perhaps I have missed you?" he suggested, cupping her elbow and moving toward the door.

"Perhaps. But there's a twinkle in your eye that has nothing to do with me."

"Ah, yes." He held the door while she passed in front of him. "Perhaps I'm in love for the last time in my life."

"Anybody I know?" She inched his ring from her finger and curled her fingers around it in the palm of her hand, afraid of what his answer might be.

"*Oui.* But not well, I think." Charles couldn't resist teasing her since he knew they'd both been blessed by finding love when they'd least expected it.

"Then you'll be needing this family heirloom, won't you?" She put the ring in his hand and watched it disappear into his jacket pocket. "Now you can tell me if the stone is a diamond."

"Would I give a beautiful woman a fake ring? Of course the stone is a diamond. While you were shopping, I was at the jeweler having the gem from an ostentatious ring my great-aunt left me mounted in something I knew you'd like." He paused beside the passenger's door of the car he'd rented. "A wish ring, my dearest friend, nothing more, nothing less."

Danielle grinned. "You're going to have to stop reading my mind unless I get the same privilege. Who's the lucky woman?"

"Isobelle Garavelli."

Her knees buckled from the unexpected news and she sank into the velour seat.

"George Garavelli's mother?" she squeaked too late. Charles had closed her door. With his cane tucked under his arm, he jauntily strode around the front of the car.

During the short drive to the restaurant, she drilled Charles with questions, but he merely smiled, chuckled, or laughed aloud. He refused to give any details.

Isobelle met them at the door. If Charles had swallowed the sun, Isobelle had swallowed the Milky Way. Charles kissed her cheeks, then grinned like a love-struck idiot.

"The chef requests your presence in the office, Danielle. There seems to be a minor problem. Dan and Ellie won't be here for an hour or so. If you'll excuse us, I'd like your friend's opinion on the table setting," Isobelle said, taking Charles by the arm and leading him toward the banquet table.

Bewildered by the turn of events, bothered by the thought of facing George, she stood motionless and watched Charles laugh at something Isobelle had murmured. Quick as a flash, he turned and winked at Danielle, then cocked his eyebrow expectantly.

She'd seen exactly the same expression on his face when Charles had asked her why she was worried about being called Bubble-butt. His raised eyebrow silently asked her if she continued to believe that a person's worth was determined by a tape measure. Was she going to let her high school perception of who

184

and what she was be an insurmountable barrier to the future?

As if to answer his questions, he turned toward Isobelle. Admiration shone in his eyes.

Neither size nor age have any bearing on falling in love, she mused, coming to grips with herself. Her hands grazed over her slender hips as she realized that Omar the Tentmaker could have designed the spangles and feathers she wore and it wouldn't make any difference to the people who loved her. The people who really cared thought she was beautiful—on the inside where it counted.

Danielle nodded. Regardless of what George thought of platonic relationships, she knew Charles would always be more than her teacher. He was a beloved friend.

With each step she took toward the kitchen, her self-confidence blossomed. In the short time she'd been in Williamsburg, she'd grown beyond Bubble-butt into a new woman.

The Garavelli brothers and Mario greeted her warmly, but looked distinctly sheepish. None of them stopped her from going toward the private office.

Worrying her bottom lip between her teeth she marched up the steps. She'd been a fool; she wasn't a coward. She'd made a dire mistake; she hadn't committed a crime. The steps she climbed were leading her to George, not the hangman's noose.

She stopped midway. Was that music she

heard coming from above? Immediately, she recognized the tune as being one from the Top Ten singles during her senior year. For a moment, curiosity replaced her dread. She slowly mounted the remainder of the steps.

Turning, what she saw made her eyes widen. The rows of cartons were gone. Blue and white crepe-paper streamers made an overhead canopy, then dangled down the wall. One table set with a single flickering candle drew her attention to a nosegay of carnations.

She had the feeling she'd stepped back in time.

George stepped from the office, dressed in a white tuxedo. He held his open palm toward her. A slight tremor passing from his hand to hers indicated his apprehension.

"We missed going to the prom together. I'm hoping we can go back to where we should have started and try again. I loved you then, but I love you now even more. Come dance with me, please?"

She felt tears gathering in her eyes, tasted their salt on her tongue. Her hand trembled as she placed it in his. Slowly, he drew her into his arms, holding her close. Her arms circled his neck as his hands settled loosely at the small of her back. His dance steps were small. They barely moved, merely swayed.

Eyes closed, she felt as though they were in a private time warp where adult problems didn't exist. Who lived where, who said what, who was right and who was wrong faded into nothingness.

"I love you, Giorgio Garavelli," she whispered. "Thank you for giving me this memory. I'll always cherish it."

"Sweet memories," he said in a hushed voice. His warm minty breath feathered across her cheek, drying the tears that refused to cease flowing. "Come live with me, Dani. Be my lover and my friend?"

Her eyes squeezed tightly. Black and white dots spiraled on a silver-gray background. Her whole body ached with love for him. "Friends?"

"The best of friends. You'll be the person I confide in. We'll share our dreams and ambitions, our anxieties and fears until there isn't any room for misunderstanding or arguments."

"Here in Williamsburg," she stated, knowing she couldn't expect him to turn his back on his business and his family.

"Wherever. I've had a dream that's almost real enough to touch. You. Me. Working together. Playing. Loving. Raising children. Growing old together. Where we make the dream reality doesn't matter."

As he spoke, Danielle mentally envisioned what he said. She wanted the same things. He'd voiced her own dream.

A silent tear clung to his eyelashes, then fell, mingling with hers. He didn't conceal it.

Tears were the dividing line between man and beast.

"Marry me, sweetheart. Soon. We've wasted too much precious time."

"Yes," she whispered. "Soon. Very soon."

The song ended, but Danielle knew the two of them would never forget the music. His lips closed over hers, softly, tenderly, a kiss to seal a memory in their hearts.

Dan and Ellie stopped bickering about the upcoming wedding long enough to take a sip of champagne from the other's glass. Mario and Buffy kissed. And Isobelle and Charles? From the secret looks they exchanged, Danielle and George knew that that was another love story.

JAYNE CASTLE

excites and delights you with tales of adventure and romance

____TRADING SECRETS

Sabrina had wanted only a casual vacation fling with the rugged Matt. But the extraordinary pull between them made that impossible. So did her growing relationship with his son—and her daring attempt to save the boy's life.
19053-3-15 $3.50

____DOUBLE DEALING

Jayne Castle sweeps you into the corporate world of multimillion dollar real estate schemes and the very private world of executive lovers. Mixing business with pleasure, they made *passion* their bottom line.
12121-3-18 $3.95

At your local bookstore or use this handy coupon for ordering:

DELL READERS SERVICE—DEPT. B1561A
6 REGENT ST., LIVINGSTON, N.J. 07039

Please send me the above title(s). I am enclosing $_____ (please add 75c per copy to cover postage and handling). Send check or money order—no cash or COQs. Please allow 3-4 weeks for shipment.
CANADIAN ORDERS: please submit in U.S. dollars.

Ms./Mrs./Mr._____

Address_____

City/State_____ Zip _____